THE UNSHAKEN MIND

THE UNSHAKEN MIND

Discovering the Purpose, Power and Potential of Your Mind

Author of the bestseller *The Source*

SIRSHREE

THE UNSHAKEN MIND

Discovering the Purpose, Power and Potential of Your Mind

By Sirshree Tejparkhi

Copyright © Tejgyan Global Foundation
All Rights Reserved 2009

Tejgyan Global Foundation is a charitable organization with its headquarters in Pune, India.

ISBN: 978-81-8415-034-6

Published by WOW Publishings Pvt. Ltd., India
Second Edition published in Jan 2014
Second reprint in November 2019

This book has been transcribed and compiled from discourses delivered by Sirshree.

Copyrights are reserved with Tejgyan Global Foundation and publishing rights are vested exclusively with WOW Publishings Pvt. Ltd. This book is sold subject to the condition that it shall not by way of trade or otherwise, be lent, resold, hired out, or otherwise circulated without the publisher's prior written consent in any form of binding or cover other than that in which it is published and without a similar condition including this condition being imposed on the subsequent purchaser and without limiting the rights under copyright reserved above, no part of this publication may be reproduced, stored in or introduced into a retrieval system, or transmitted, in any form, or by any means, electronic, mechanical, photocopying, recording or otherwise, without the prior written permission of both the copyright owner and the above-mentioned publisher of this book. Any person who does any unauthorized act in relation to this publication may be liable to criminal prosecution and civil claims for damages.

Although the author and publisher have made every effort to ensure accuracy of content in this book, they hereby disclaim any liability to any party for any loss, damage, or disruption caused by errors or omissions, resulting from negligence, accident, or any other cause. Readers are advised to take full responsibility to exercise discretion in understanding and applying the content of this book.

*To those compilers,
whose meticulous efforts of compiling the sayings of
great masters and thinkers has helped preserve and
string together the scattered pearls of wisdom,
keeping them ever fresh in the minds of people.*

Contents

	Preface	ix
1.	What is the Mind?	3
2.	The Types of the Mind	6
3.	The Contrast Mind	14
4.	How to See the Mind	21
5.	Taking Credit	26
6.	Churning	30
7.	Deceit	34
8.	Labelling	38
9.	Mission Earth	47
10.	Why Train the Mind	50
11.	Set Goals and Time Limits	56
12.	Enquire About the Mind	62
13.	Concentrate the Mind	69
14.	Pray and Meditate	75

15.	Purify the Mind	79
16.	Employ the Mind in Selfless Service	85
17.	Energize the Mind	89
18.	Safeguard the Mind	96
19.	Move Your Mind	101
20.	Engage Your Mind in Creativity	106
21.	Transcending the Mind	115
22.	Train the Inner Mind	122
23.	Immerse the Mind in Devotion	127
24.	Sublimate the Mind Through Self-Expression	135
25.	If You Have Faith, You Will See	139
26.	The Mind is Not the Seer, But the Sight	144
27.	Silence the Mind	150
28.	Questions and Answers	154

Preface

Let there be Faith in the mind; Let Love reside therein;
Then you will be successful forever.

From time immemorial, man is troubled by the whims and fancies of his mind. The mind is like a pendulum which continuously oscillates between pairs of opposites such as past and future, happiness and sorrow, success and failure. It rarely remains in the present. In order to be in the present, the mind needs to do 'nothing' and that is the most difficult thing for the mind. Even if the mind is asked to do 'nothing', it tries to 'do' nothing. It always wants to do something.

Musicians love to be lost in the peak of musical performance. Likewise, athletes like being in the thick of activity. Consider the example of a pianist who is lost in playing a piano. When his performance is at its peak, he is lost in the performance. It is as if he does not exist then. Where is his mind when this is happening? His mind has dropped momentarily. But once the performance is over, the mind returns to claim that it was present during the performance.

The real joy that the musician or the athlete experiences is because the mind drops and they experience the present moment. However, they generally do so without the right understanding.

They believe that it is the musical performance or the athletic activity that is giving them joy. Without the right understanding, they continue to seek the joy of the present moment through external means. However, the source of joy is not in the gross external world. Whenever the mind drops, we are in the present—in timeless existence. But, one may wonder how the mind can drop, when it always wants to do something.

The mind when focussed in the external world and properly guided can help us acquire knowledge, power and the possessions of this world. If the mind is trained to focus within, it can help unleash the latent powers and possibilities within us. Further, if the mind is trained to attain the highest purpose for which we are born, it can support this endeavour completely to the extent that it will even dissolve itself in the process. If the mind can be trained to be the very cause for joy, then why should one undergo the sufferings of this mind? One would rather start with the training immediately!

The mind gets deluded in the mire of illusion. It becomes impure with tendencies and patterns. Such a mind becomes a hindrance in one's progress. Man has tried several techniques and remedies to win over his mind. When he tries to suppress this mind, the mind can fall into the depth of depression. When the mind is given freedom, it can rise to the height of arrogance. It can become stubborn and indulge in gratification of its insatiable desires by all possible means. Hence it is essential to understand what this mind is, its behavioural tendencies, and its functioning. It is important to learn techniques to train this mind and use the mind for the attainment of the highest purpose of human life.

This book throws light on all these aspects. The book is divided into four sections.

The first section is about knowing the mind. This section

explores what the mind is. It delves into the different types of mind.

The second section throws light on how to perceive the mind. It discusses certain traits of the mind that pose a hurdle in winning over the mind.

The third section deals with how the mind can be trained to attain Mission Earth – the very purpose of the life.

The fourth section explains how the mind can be transcended.

Whether you are new to this subject or have prior knowledge about the mind, this book can surely assist in training your mind. A lot has been written on the subject of the mind, dealing with its scientific aspects. However, this book is different. It reveals the spiritual reality of the mind. It imparts the techniques to master the mind and further transcend it. This will help unleash our latent possibilities. It can help us lead a life of bliss and equanimity.

Wish you all the best to get the best from this book!

Part One

About the Mind Knowing it!

1
What is the Mind?

The mind is a good friend when there is no attachment. It is a bad enemy if it is your master. Use the mind. Do not become its slave.

There are some things in this world which we cannot see with our eyes. We can only feel their existence. Our feelings make us believe their existence. This is also true with the mind. We cannot see the mind. However, when we sense that something is happening, then we sense its existence. It is similar to air. We cannot see air. But when we see leaves fluttering in the wind, we realize the presence of air.

The mind - a bundle of thoughts

To understand what exactly the mind is, consider the example of a woollen sweater. If we consistently keep pulling the woollen thread of the sweater, then very soon we will find that the so called object named sweater no longer exists. It merely remains as a woollen thread. What we perceived as a sweater was an illusion. The mind too is an illusion which is created by thoughts. Thus, the answer to the question what is the mind is that it is a bundle of thoughts. Thought is the thread of the mind with which it is knitted. The mind is actually just thoughts and nothing else. If there are no thoughts, there is no mind. In the absence of thoughts, silence alone prevails.

The mind is forever busy in its work of comparing, dividing and weighing. What should we bind this mind with so that it starts functioning in the right manner? How can it get free from its entanglements, attachments and stubbornness to get things done in its own way? The mind may feel temporarily relieved. However, no sooner does the mind get another chance, it starts playing by its whims.

Where does the mind live?

The mind is a medium for exchange of thoughts. It is a union of thoughts. Wherever we pay attention, thoughts connected to the subject start building up in the mind. If you are thinking about a garden, your mind immediately reaches there. It starts imagining about the garden and thoughts pertaining to that arise. In this way, the mind is where the attention is. The answer to the question - Where is the mind? - is that it is where attention is. A question may arise - Where is the mind in the body? Is it in the brain? The brain is a tool, an organ that the mind uses. Just now if someone were to ask you, "Where is your mind?", you might say, "It is in my eyes." Your focus is on your eyes as you read this. But your brain was used to process the information. An answer to the question where is the mind in the body is that the mind is everywhere in the body. And your brain is used to process a thought that originates in the mind.

Looking behind the stream of thoughts

When thoughts stop arising at night, we fall asleep. But thoughts again become active during dreams. It is the mind which weaves this intricate web of thoughts. There is no gap between any of these thoughts. They are constantly linked to one another. This stream of thoughts is flowing forever. As soon as one thought ends, another one starts. This can be understood through an example.

A person needs to reach his office. He is heading to take the bus. The first thought occurs to him, "I hope I reach the bus stop on time." When he reaches the bus stop, the next thought occurs, "I hope the bus arrives on time." Once the bus arrives, and he gets into the bus, the next thought occurs, "I hope to get a place to sit." After he gets a place to sit, the next thought arises, "I must reach office on time." In this way, there is a continuous stream of thoughts that constantly flows in the mind which seems unstoppable.

Now, imagine that you are waiting on a platform at the train station. A train is passing by. You are interested to know what is lying on the adjoining platform. While the train is passing by, your focus is on the empty gaps between the compartments of the train to get a glimpse of the object kept on the other side.

In the same way, even though thoughts are incessantly running, with meditation you can focus in the gaps between the two consecutive thoughts. With consistent practice of meditation, these empty spaces slowly begin to grow, and the mind disappears in the end. Then what remains is silence. This silence from where thoughts originate is Consciousness – a state of beingness.

What Next?

Further chapters ahead in the book will help you understand how to transcend the mind. But before that, let us look at the types of the mind in the next chapter.

2
The Types of the Mind

Whatever thoughts we sleep with at night, ruminate in the subconscious mind. Therefore, always inspire yourself with positive thoughts and truth thoughts before you go to sleep.

To understand the mind better, this chapter categorizes the mind into different types based on its functions and the state of the mind. Let us go through these categories.

Categorization based on the functions of the mind

1. The inner mind and the outer mind

The inner mind is also referred as the subconscious mind or the unconscious mind. The outer mind is the outwardly focused conscious mind. The difference between them is as vast as the difference between a breeze and a storm. The working of the conscious mind is visible; while that of the subconscious mind is invisible. The subconscious mind works silently. While, the conscious mind sees and experiences every feeling and thought, makes judgments, jumps to conclusions and is restless.

The conscious mind is responsible for all actions performed by the sense organs like reading, sitting, walking, writing, seeing, hearing, etc. All the thoughts arise from the inner mind. When such a thought comes at the level of the conscious mind, we perceive that such a thought has arisen. From an operational point of view, it can be said that 10% of the mind is the conscious mind and the remaining 90% is the subconscious mind.

All involuntary functions of the body like breathing, heart beats, digestion of food, controlling blood circulation are managed by the inner mind. Our inner mind is also involved in situations where several movements are made by our body unconsciously. For example, when we are sitting at one place, when we automatically pull a blanket to cover our body while we are asleep. In order to have an undisturbed sleep at night, the inner mind shows strange dreams. For example, if we are feeling thirsty, then the inner mind shows a dream in which we are drinking water, or a scene of a river or the sea is shown to us. In the same way, if we are fast asleep and there is a loud noise outside, the inner mind shows a dream in which someone rings our doorbell. The inner mind does all this so that we can sleep uninterruptedly. The inner mind has immense power.

Our inner or subconscious mind works according to the instructions received from the outer or conscious mind; however the true control room is in the subconscious mind. It does not distinguish between right and wrong. The subconscious mind also does not understand the difference between imaginary and real. It merely executes the thoughts provided by the conscious mind. If our subconscious mind receives a wrong instruction – in this case, thoughts – such as, "I can fall ill", "I am poor", "I can fail", the subconscious mind begins attracting such outcomes in life. Hence, it is crucial to be always aware of our thoughts. We need to watch what messages we are sending to our inner mind.

Both these minds are necessary for the functioning of the body.

There is no question of one being superior to the other. Both are important, and both have significant roles to play. However, it is essential to note that Consciousness is more important than both the conscious mind and the subconscious mind. Consciousness is beyond both the conscious and subconscious mind. Consciousness is the life force because of which the mind operates in the first place. Because we are alive, the outer mind functions. It in turn gives instructions to the inner mind. Consciousness is like electricity which provides the electric charge that lights the bulb. The bulb is worthless without electricity. The bulb is our body and mind.

2. The contrast mind and the intuitive mind

Contrast mind is the contrasting, comparing, judging mind. The intuitive mind is also referred as instinctive mind, simple mind. When the mind gets into comparison, judgement, measurement, calculations then it is called the contrast mind. This mind invariably divides everything into two. It has the habit of differentiating everything into black or white, good or bad, success or failure, right or wrong. It always comments on whatever happens. When something happens, it immediately concludes whether it was good or bad, whether this should have or should not have happened. The contrast mind takes a lot of interest in such worthless things. Apart from such things, it has no other work to do.

Unless we get liberated from the contrast mind, we will be entangled in the perpetual cycles of joy and sorrow all our lives. The calculating thoughts of the contrast mind keep on troubling the human mind. This is one of the reasons why people resort to sleeping pills at night to get sleep. Once this calculative contrast mind is won over, man can experience the supreme bliss. The contrast mind is the major roadblock in the attainment of the state of happiness. The state of happiness has always been there since the beginning. As soon as the contrast mind drops, Consciousness becomes aware of itself.

Unlike the contrast mind, the intuitive mind just does the work given to it. It does not differentiate between black and white. While driving a car, the intuitive mind will instruct when the car needs to be turned, where it needs to be stopped. Thoughts like "This is my work", "This is someone else's work" are not entertained by this mind. When we are completely immersed in work, the intuitive mind draws some things from our memory bank. If we have learnt some things about that work in the past, then the intuitive mind draws that information from the past references in our memory bank. It makes use of that information to get the present tasks done in the best possible manner.

Let us understand how the intuitive mind functions through an example. Consider a situation where you are driving a car, and suddenly a bicycle comes in your way. At that moment, you do not think, "If I take a right turn, there are children playing there. So let me turn left. There is a large puddle on the left side. So let me apply breaks now." At that time, without even thinking you just apply the brakes to stop the car. This is the intuitive mind. Later on, when you describe this event to your friends, you say, "While I was driving the car, someone came on my way. I could not swerve to the right as children were playing there. Neither could I turn the car to the left, as there was a large puddle. So I just applied the brakes and stopped." Now, this entire narration came from your memory. This is your contrast mind in operation. Ask this contrast mind who applied the brakes – was it explicitly done by the contrast mind or brakes got applied intuitively? When the actual secret is revealed, then the mind becomes free of ego.

A painter draws a picture using his intuitive mind. While drawing the picture, his intuitive mind thinks, "Let us explore with this colour this time." On the other hand, the contrast mind thinks, "Drawings are not appreciated these days. Will this picture be sold?" As soon as the contrast mind becomes active, the trouble starts. Ego is born due to the contrast mind. Ego is the false 'I'. It is the false sense of 'self' which always remains unhappy and troubled.

The intuitive mind is always in the present while the contrast mind is in the past or the future.

3. P-F mind and present mind

The contrast mind lives either in tomorrow or yesterday. It dwells either in the past, which has already happened, or the future, which is yet to happen. Hence, it is playfully referred as the P-F (past/future) mind.

Think about the school days when every Sunday was a holiday. Which was your happier day at that time – Saturday or Sunday? It was Saturday after the school was over. You would invariably think, "Tomorrow is Sunday. It's a holiday." But on Sunday, you would think, "Tomorrow is Monday. Need to go to school tomorrow." This is the P-F mind. It lives either in the past or the future and destroys the pleasures of the present. It just cannot stay in the present.

Generally, people enjoy a lot when they are busy in making preparations for festivals like Diwali or Christmas. But, on the actual day of the festival they say, "This year's Diwali is not that exciting. Last year's Diwali or Christmas was better." Why does this happen? It happens because as soon as the present moment arrives, the P-F mind either jumps into the future or the past. One needs to turn this P-F mind into a present mind.

The present mind as the name suggests is one that is always in the present. The present is whatever is happening around us right now. The mind that keeps watching what is happening now is the present mind. When we learn to watch whatever is happening in the present from a witness point of view in its entirety, then we master the art of living in the present.

It is not being said that one should not think about the past or the future at all. To learn from mistakes of the past, let the mind visit the past and quickly return to the present. But there is no need to remain stuck in the past. Similarly, for foresight, let the mind peep into the future and return. There is no need to dwell in the future for a long period of time.

Categorization based on the state of a trained mind

An untrained mind is a slave of the contrast mind or the P-F mind. Let us understand the states of a trained mind.

1. Plus Mind

At the basic level, the mind has to be trained to remain positive. A mind, thus trained, is referred as a Plus mind, symbolized by the '+' sign. The plus mind always harbours positive thoughts. The mind that dwells in negativity needs to be trained to entertain positive thoughts, so as to achieve the ultimate purpose of life. We need to make ourselves plus-minded first. These positive thoughts will then create a doorway to develop a pure mind.

2. Pure Mind

A pure mind is one which is free from hatred, spite, ill-will, envy and jealousy. Such a mind does not harm anyone. There are people who train the mind, so as to attain mystical powers. However, merely training the mind to gain such powers is not enough. The power of purity and benevolence is essential to ensure that the mind serves the wellbeing of society. The practice of forbearance and forgiveness lends purity to the mind. A pure mind alone can be used to attain the purpose of our lives.

3. Peaceful mind

When the pure mind becomes peaceful, then it becomes instrumental to spread peace everywhere. All countries in the world aspire for a peaceful environment. However, peace initiatives do not bear fruit due to the presence of ill-will and vested interests amongst leaders. When the pure mind begins to love and embrace peace in daily life, then it becomes instrumental for spreading peace in society.

4. Devoted mind.

A devoted mind is one that is surrendered to Consciousness. Later chapters in this book will explore how to transcend the mind to be established in Consciousness. When the mind is filled with divine devotion, selfless service and complete surrender to Consciousness, then it is a devoted mind. In the Indian epic, the *Ramayana*, Hanuman is portrayed as an ardent devotee of Lord Rama. Hanuman is considered to be the epitome of service, devotion and complete surrender to the truth. This is a depiction of a devoted mind. The words used to describe this state of mind do not matter. If your mind gets established in the present, then all activities in your life will be accomplished with joy and devotion. Your mind will become a devoted mind. Such a mind will then become peaceful, pure and ready to surrender to Consciousness. Such a mind invites the no-mind state so that Consciousness is revealed to itself.

5. No-mind

No-mind is a state where the mind is thoughtless. To achieve this state, it is essential that the mind is free from all unwanted thoughts. Once the mind surrenders itself, Consciousness is revealed to itself. However, when the mind refuses to surrender because of its stubbornness and ego, then sorrow, darkness and misery spreads everywhere. By practicing meditation, we can attain the no-mind state.

Once a seeker attains a no-mind state, the mind may return. That is when it is important to be in devotion. In order to be established in Consciousness, either a no-mind state or a devoted mind is required.

What Next?

The biggest hindrance to go beyond the mind and be established in Consciousness is the contrast mind. In the next chapter, we will learn about the contrast mind in more detail.

3
The Contrast Mind

When the mind abides in the present, it is called the intuitive mind. But when it is filled with thoughts of comparison and judgement, this same mind is referred as the contrast mind.

A sage was sitting by the side of a river when a jeweller approached him. With great reverence, he offered two diamonds to the sage. Since the jeweller had recently made some good profits, it was easy for him to part with the two diamonds.

When the jeweller was handing over the diamonds to the sage, the sage's hands shook a little. One of the diamonds slipped off his hands and fell into the river. The jeweller saw it. He immediately dived in the river to retrieve it. But it was of no use. The current was too strong. The jeweller could not recover it from the flowing waters. He came up and asked the sage, "O holy sage! I could not retrieve the diamond. You were sitting by the riverside. Can you please tell me the exact place where the diamond dropped into the water?" The sage took the second diamond in his hand and threw it into the water and said, "The first diamond fell right there!"

The jeweller's heart was broken when the first diamond was lost, and the sage dropped the second diamond as well. What made it so easy for the sage to throw the second diamond? There has to be some reason, some understanding behind this. The intuitive mind of the sage was predominant. Therefore, loss of both the diamonds did not cause any sorrow to him. However, in case of the jeweller, his contrast mind was in force at that time. Therefore, he could not bear the loss of the diamonds, although he had already parted with them and offered them to the sage.

As you have already seen earlier, the contrast mind is perpetually comparing. It constantly engages itself in comparison and judgement. It is the root cause of all unhappiness.

The contrast mind and the 'I' thought

The first thought that comes to our mind as we wake up in the morning is the 'I' thought. For example, "I have woken up. I have got up. What is the first thing I should do? There is still heaviness in my eyes. Is it the right time for me to wake up?" The words could be different, but all of them revolve around the word 'I'. Following this 'I' thought, all other thoughts start arising and by then all the sense organs become active. The contrast mind comes into existence after the 'I' thought. It now starts evaluating everything all the time whether it was good or bad.

This mind considers itself to be separate from everything else and lives accordingly. It distinguishes everything as my work, my name, my deeds, my religion, my country, my sins, my virtues. By thinking that "I am different from others" it gives rise to ego. In this way, it keeps evaluating every thought that has occurred. It keeps judging every incident which takes place. It keeps vacillating in situations of happiness and unhappiness. This is the cause of all misery and bondage.

Impact of the contrast mind in humans

When a lion chases a deer, the deer runs for its life. After sometime, it somehow manages to get out of sight of the lion. It gets relieved. The very next moment it is grazing on the grass fields. Is the deer complaining about its fate, "Why am I made this way? Why should I be victimized and fall a prey to such beasts?" It never has any such concerns. Once, the incident is over, the deer moves on with the next incident. It has forgotten whatever was happening just a few moments ago. It does not have any thoughts as it does not have a contrast mind.

There is no contrast mind in animals. There is only intuitive mind in animals. However, as the contrast mind functions in humans, there is a different experience. After every incident, the contrast mind continuously keeps weighing things. It comments, "He should not have behaved like this with me", "He did it on purpose", "I know it", "Why does this happen with me?", "Why do I get angry with people from the other territory?" We get angry on the fact that we got angry. We need to stop getting angry on our anger.

The contrast mind results in misery. The contrast mind pushes some things away from it and pulls some things towards it. It tries to run away from those things which it dislikes and tries to run after those things which it likes. It constantly engages itself in this struggle. It craves for pleasure and has an aversion for pain. It not only battles with unhappiness but also with happiness. It is worried of not losing the happiness. Life never unfolds in its entirety in front of us. It unfolds only in parts. But, the contrast mind tries to judge the entire story looking at these small parts.

The contrast mind also results in guilt. It remembers past events by retrieving the information stored in memory. If it judges a past event as a mistake or a blunder, the contrast mind creates a feeling of guilt. Some people spend their entire lives being steeped in the feeling of guilt.

The contrast mind does not allow the mind to be in the present. It vacillates between what has happened in the past and what will happen in the future. As a result, it moves out of the present moment.

The intuitive mind vs. The contrast mind

When the mind is focused in the present with thoughts of carrying out the current task, it is called the intuitive mind. When it is filled with thoughts of comparison and judgement, it is called the contrast mind. When the thoughts focus in one direction, they remind us of our goal. When the thoughts are centred on the individual – the 'I' thought – it gives birth to the ego. The contrast mind survives on thoughts of the past and the future. The intuitive mind uses the intellect as a tool to help us take decisions.

The contrast mind looks at everything from an individualistic perspective. It comments, "It is my work." When the work is accomplished successfully, it says, "Wow! What a great achievement… I have done it!" When it fails, then it laments, "Oh! I failed miserably." If it is not able to perform, it is anxious, "What will happen to me now? I have made such silly mistakes."

It tries to take stock of all the happy events from the past and imagines the happy events that it fancies for the future. While doing so, it also wants to be sure about whether the happy events will happen or not. It feels that nothing can be achieved without its thinking. It comes up with the list of tasks to be done in the present and the future. It gets the feeling of carrying a big burden of work. It tries to manage all the tasks. Unless it is clear about their plan of execution, it does not start working on it. It believes that life can be beautiful only after it acquires certain things or when its existing problem is resolved. It treats itself to be special and different from others. It complains, "Things are limited and too many people are there to stake a claim on it. Everyone will not have it."

It is only when the contrast mind loosens its hold that the intuitive mind gets an opportunity to function. The intuitive mind functions in the most natural way with ease. It does not tag labels like good or bad. You can see that your intuitive mind does most of the work in a day. The contrast mind intervenes in between and spoils the work. It can do enough damage even if it gets a few moments. For example, if your neighbour walks into your house and abuses or belittles you, your entire day can be spoiled due to the commentary of the contrast mind.

When the intuitive mind plays its role, an incident occurs and instantly ends. However, the same incident lingers and turns into an unhappy one, if the contrast mind comes into play. Thus, it is important to learn to tame the contrast mind. But before we do that, let us explore how to see the mind in its various facets in the next section of the book.

What Next?

The next section discusses how to see the mind and explains the four key traits of the mind.

Part Two

Seeing the Mind Sensing it!

4

How to See the Mind

An impure mind is sorrow; a pure mind is happiness;
but a no-mind is 'bright happiness'.

Just like the mind is of different types according to the different facets it holds, it has several vices too. In the Indian epic, the Ramayana, the demon Ravana had ten heads. The mind also has ten horrifying faces such as anger, boredom, comparison, depression, ego, fear, greed, hatred, ill-will and envy. It can be said that the mind exists because of these vices or the mind exists and so are the vices present.

The shifting mind

The mind is unstable by nature. It constantly keeps vacillating all the time. It constantly keeps changing its states. If it is filled with envy in the morning, it changes to anger in the afternoon, in the evening it is full of greed, and at night it is confused. The mind changes every moment. At one moment, it feels dejected, and at the other moment it is happy. At one moment, it is happy, and at the other moment it is unhappy. It is filled with trust a moment before, and the very next moment distrust and doubt seeps in. Just now it is filled with reverence, but the very next moment it is full of deceit. A little while ago, it was compassionate but right now it is full of anger. A moment ago it was ready to die for someone, but the next moment it might be ready to kill the same person. Thus, one cannot trust this ever-changing mind. The biggest irony is that we have got identified with this unstable mind. We have tremendous faith and trust on this unstable mind.

Mind – an illusion

The mind is an illusion *(maya)*. An illusion is that which is not actually present but appears real. Although the mind does not exist, it makes you feel it real. You can compare the illusory nature of the mind to a stick that is dipped in water. Though it appears to be bent, in reality the stick is not bent. When you see a rope in the dark, it appears like a snake. Similarly, the mind too appears to be real due to ignorance, but it does not exist. To understand this mind, one needs to look at it in the light of wisdom.

The mind comes into existence when we identify ourselves with it. As soon as we think, "I am the body, I am the mind", the mind comes into existence. Though we may not explicitly say or think such thoughts, these form the underlying notions and beliefs that give rise to derived thoughts. We become whatever we identify with. If we identify with the religion, we become a Hindu, or a Muslim, or a Christian. If we identify with the professional role we play, we become that role such as doctor, engineer, painter, carpenter, etc. If we identify with wealth, we become rich. Whatever we attach the 'I' thought to, we become that.

For example, the moment a bride gets married to a bridegroom, all his relatives become hers. A moment ago the bride did not have any of those relationships. But, a moment later all the relationships came into existence. Similarly, the moment we identify with the mind, all its vices such as anger, lust, envy, ill-will, comparison, jealousy, confusion, dejection, happiness, unhappiness, enmity, friendship, anguish, success, failure, etc become ours.

Diving into the mind's vices

Desire is the most important and formidable weapon of the untrained mind. This is manifested in terms of craving, yearning or lust. The mind that is untrained derives its life force from it. Desire keeps it alive. The mind continuously and consistently triggers desires. When desires are not fulfilled, the untrained mind becomes angry. If the desires are fulfilled, greed takes over. When the untrained mind acquires the objects of its desires, it develops attachment for those objects and fear of losing them. This gives rise to the tendency of accumulation. It further gives rise to ego. In this way, the chain of bondage of the mind is formed by joining of various links. If any of these links is weakened with understanding, then this bondage of the mind can weaken and break.

But the key question is why does desire arise. It arises because the mind labels things as good or bad. It arises because of the tendency of the mind to churn and compare between the past and the future, between good and bad. It arises because the mind likes to take credit. It also arises because the mind does not tell the truth to itself. So there are deeper habits or traits that are behind the ones that are apparent.

Seeing the mind

Among many vices and traits including desire, there are four specific traits of the untrained mind that need special attention. These four traits are: the habit of taking credit, the habit of churning, the habit of deceit and the habit of labelling. The contrast mind stands tall on these four legs. Once we understand these legs of the mind, we start seeing the mind for what it is. Liberation from the mind then becomes easier. There are also other legs or habits of the contrast mind. But, these four are suggested as the primary ones leading to all the negative traits and vices of the mind.

The way to see the mind is to notice these negative habits arising in the mind. These habits are the source of all negative traits. Hence, the focus is on these four. Just notice and tell yourself – this thought is arising because of the habit of deceit, this thought is occurring because of the habit of taking credit, etc. In the chapters that follow in this section, understand each of these traits. New concepts such as 'churning' or 'labelling' will also become clear.

Practical Exercise

The following exercise helps you see the contrast mind and notice the difference between the intuitive mind and the contrast mind. Close your eyes and assign a number to every incoming breath. Begin with 1 and increase the count with each breath. If your mind wanders away, then slowly bring it back and restart with 1. If you are able to do so with closed eyes, now practice with open eyes. Continue counting every incoming breath. If you are able to do it with open eyes, then continue the exercise by standing up. Now start moving about and continue the exercise.

After having done this for a few minutes, stop doing the exercise. Contemplate on the thoughts that arose when you did the exercise. Thoughts such as "This is the breath", "This is 1", etc. are all thoughts from the intuitive mind. All other thoughts, specially ones to do with past or future, good or bad, thoughts that are commentary on what is happening – are all thoughts of the contrast mind. This exercise not only helps you to understand the contrast mind, but also helps in training the mind not to wander away by being influenced by the contrast mind.

What Next?

Let us now look at the first negative habit of the untrained mind of taking credit in the next chapter.

5
Taking Credit

Just as a spider spins a web from its own mouth and remains entangled in it, so also does the mind that applies negative logic keeps getting entangled in its own net.

The habit of taking unnecessary credit is behind many of the mind's vices. As a part of our mind's training, it is essential that we train our mind to stop taking credit. Let us first look at what taking credit means. Taking credit means claiming something without having done anything. Whatever has happened so far in our lives has happened naturally and spontaneously. The intuitive mind played its role at that time. But after the incident, the contrast mind comes to the fore and claims the credit.

Craving for praise

Contemplate on your life. Think about the past ten incidents of your life. Ask yourself how they happened. Did you have to do anything for that, or they just happened automatically? You will realize that the events just happened naturally. For example, when you get up in the morning, do you think of getting up or you just get up? You will find that you just get up in the morning. It happens spontaneously.

Look at the most trivial as well as the major incidents in your life and the way they happened. You will realize that they happened automatically, naturally and spontaneously. But the mind wants to take credit for all that has happened. Why does it want credit? This is because the mind wants to be appreciated and praised for whatever has happened. Why does it want to be praised and appreciated? Who we truly are – beyond the mind – is complete in itself. However, as we identify with our mind and body, we consider ourselves separate from everything else. Being unaware of our essential nature of completeness, we seek completeness by gaining praise and appreciation.

When the mind takes the credit, then it gets recognition from others. We are not likely to get any praise from others if we say, "I do not know how it happened. It is a wonder for me too. I never knew that such thoughts would occur to me, and I would speak those words. How can I claim credit for that? I did not do anything."

The mind is a slave of praise. There is an overflow of infinite joy within each one of us. Happiness sought from appreciation and praise is a false happiness. We need not have to replenish it with the happiness derived out of false external praise. Instead of entangling ourselves in false happiness, we should kindle the inner quest for true happiness. When the mind gains understanding and learns to look within, then it stops taking credit. It stops looking for praise.

The mind - a servant without a job

The contrast mind is like a servant without any work to do. It always gives its opinion as this is good; this is bad. It tries to take credit for everything. If you stop giving credit to it, the role of the contrast mind diminishes. Even if the contrast mind does arise, you will tell it, "Both 'doing' as well as 'not doing' is not in your hands. You have never done anything. Everything has happened spontaneously." The contrast mind does not accept this easily as it desperately seeks credit. Therefore, it will come back again in different forms by presenting its case logically. It will say, "See, nowadays I have stopped taking credit." At this time, we need to tell the mind, "It is good that you are not taking credit. But you do not have to take credit for not taking credit either." In this way, repeatedly give this understanding to the mind and lead it to the feeling of acceptance and gratitude.

Once the mind gains understanding about the truth, its habit of constantly seeking praise gradually breaks. When the desire for the subtlest praise also diminishes, then the ego starts melting. Thereafter, the true surrender of the mind happens where there is no ego. As there is no ego, there is no one to take credit of the surrender. True surrender happens only with understanding. At this time, a strong conviction arises that nothing happens without the thoughts given by the Self – our true nature. The mind stops taking credit after realization of the truth. From this point onwards, a sublime sense of gratitude prevails, and the mind simply dissolves in this feeling of gratitude.

The key reason behind not taking credit

The reason to avoid the habit of taking credit is not just to make the mind not hanker for praise. There is a deeper meaning to it which we will consider in the section on Transcending the Mind. At a deeper level, the question is not as much about why the mind seeks credit, but rather a more profound question of where thoughts arise from. To this day, we have believed that we bring forth thoughts. However, the truth is: We don't bring thoughts. Thoughts arise from the inner source, from Consciousness. After a thought arises from the Source, the untrained mind churns many more thoughts around it. From one thought, the mind produces more thoughts that lead an individual to feel, "I did this." A thought arises from the Source and an action happens through the body. If that thought does not arise, there will not be any action by the body. Thus training the mind for not taking credit is not only helpful in avoiding various vices, but more importantly it is the basis for transcending the mind to be established in the Source.

How to train the mind not to take credit

Notice when the mind takes credit, how it takes credit for trivial matters as well as major happenings. Just notice and report to yourself. Notice how the mind may take credit by saying, "Nowadays, I don't take credit at all." Notice the undercurrents of the subtle ego – "How spiritual I am!"

Practical Exercise

Be seated for sometime and watch what is happening within. See how a thought occurs to you and you get into action. After every action, the mind tries to take credit – I have done it. But, tell yourself, "Doing and not doing is not in my hands. Everything is happening spontaneously and automatically." Watch the next thought that occurs within you. Continue with this exercise for 10 minutes.

What Next?

Having looked at the first major trait of the contrast mind, we will now explore the second trait of the mind – Churning.

6
Churning

Thoughts of past and future are the food on which the contrast mind thrives. Intellect is the tool of the intuitive mind which helps us take decisions.

Let us examine the habit of churning of the mind. Churning is similar to what acrobats do in a circus. They perform somersaults or cartwheels.

For example, a thought emerges, "Guests will visit in the evening." Then a whole lot of churning thoughts follow – "Oh! I will have to arrange for their food. The fridge is empty. These guests are fussy. They would expect only homemade food. What will happen if they get upset? etc."

Why to stop churning?

A man who was injured in an accident was immediately rushed to the hospital. During those moments, he could only think of reaching the hospital at the earliest and quickly get treated. After reaching the hospital, he was sedated and underwent surgery. Soon after he regained his consciousness, his contrast mind got into its act. It started with its churning. Thoughts gushed up, "Will I be able to work with this injured hand? How will I complete my pending tasks? Now, I will not be able to do anything. If I will not do it, then who else will do it? What will happen to my job? What will happen if I become jobless?" With this churning of the mind, trouble, worry and unhappiness slowly crept in. When the accident happened, the contrast mind was absent. The intuitive mind alone was present and it performed its role beautifully. But after the incident happened, the contrast mind came into picture and started with its churning. It gave birth to misery.

Thus, churning of thoughts happens in some people perhaps for an hour, in others for five hours, in some for even many days together. Longer the churning, greater is the sorrow.

The habit of churning is the basis for various negative traits of the mind such as anger, worry, depression, greed, lust, boredom, fear, jealousy, ill-will, etc.

Everything happens spontaneously, easily and naturally. We go through every incident spontaneously. But after the incident happens, the contrast mind comes to the fore and then the trouble starts.

Specially let negative churning stop

The untrained mind twists, turns and churns in every incident. On every negative thought, it feels that something bad is going to happen. It then starts churning over that, "This should not happen. That should not occur." For example, suppose that you are driving your car peacefully on a road. Suddenly thoughts occur, "I hope my car does not meet with an accident. I hope my car does not breakdown somewhere." In this way, the contrast mind goes on with its churning for a long time. Then you safely reach home only to discover that those thoughts were there just as a matter of precaution and nothing as such happened. The mind just wanted to warn you for safe driving but gave rise to so many thoughts along with it. All these thoughts were meaningless and futile. They scared you and made you anxious. You will realize it properly when you will gain an understanding about it.

Now, as soon as thoughts arise in your mind, learn to re-affirm yourself, "The mind is going to do churning on this thought. But, I will not get stuck in this." With this affirmation, the churning, which was about to start on that thought, would stop. Then another thought may arise. Again, you need to stop the churning which would have begun with that thought.

Stop churning to also transcend the mind

The first thought invariably arises from Consciousness, the Source. The first thought is like a straight vertical line. It takes no time for this thought to occur. Following this thought, the churning of the mind goes on for a long time which is like a horizontal line.

Getting into churning is a trait of the untrained mind. The more churning the mind does, the stronger it becomes. Churning is the food for the mind. When you stop the churning, you are in effect starving the untrained mind.

So now, with this awareness, the horizontal thoughts will diminish. When the horizontal line of thoughts is stopped, then your life would become a straight vertical line. Thereafter, you will start living in the present and enjoy everlasting happiness.

Practical Exercise

Close your eyes and remain seated in a meditative posture. As soon as a thought arises in your mind, re-affirm to yourself, "The mind is going to engage in some churning on this thought. But, I will not get stuck with this." With this affirmation, the churning, which was about to start on that thought, would stop. Then another thought may arise. In this way, continue with the exercise for 10 minutes.

What Next?

In the next chapter, we will examine the third negative habit of the mind – deceit.

7

Deceit

Sorrow is just an indication given to us that now it is time to make our mind pure, surrendered, peaceful and unshakable.

What is the truth of deceit – the lies of the mind? Deceit is when our feelings, thoughts, words and actions are not aligned.

Imagine a situation where you come across one of your friends whom you have not met since long. You tell him that you have been thinking about calling him. Though you know that you have some important work the next day, yet you promise him that you will surely meet him the next day at leisure. If you promise him this just for the sake of it without really meaning what you said, then this is deceit. This example shows how your feelings, thoughts, words and actions are not aligned with each other.

The truth behind deceit

Deceit is the food of the mind. To hide is deceit. To hide partly in your speech is deceit. To exaggerate is deceit. To beat around the bush is deceit. To delay or avoid answering, even when you know the answer or the right thing to do, is deceit. When you resolve to speak only truth, you do not need to remember or worry about what you said yesterday or a week ago or a month ago. Saying one thing a month ago and another thing a month later is deceit. This is how the untrained mind survives.

Deceit is when you exaggerate or hide the truth. One may complain, "I might have told my friend at least fifty times how to get things right, but this friend of mine just does not get it." In this example, did this person really tell his friend fifty times? Probably not! But the mind's habit of exaggeration makes him or her say that. Similarly, people hide the truth about themselves due to fear of being ridiculed. There is no reason to be scared and lie to avoid being ridiculed.

Awareness of deceit sets you free

When you are aware of these unnecessary lies, when you understand how the mind uses the trait of deceit, you will at least stop these unnecessary deceits. When you are aware of this habit of the mind and do not engage in deceit, the untrained mind will have no space to hide.

Examine all your relationships to see if there is deceit. If you carefully examine your relationships, you might observe that there is some level of deceit among friends and relatives just because you do not want them to be upset with you. There is exaggeration or hiding in what you say to them or what they tell you. There is deceit between a husband and a wife too. The husband tells his wife that the train leaves at 5:45 pm. But the actual time of the train is at 6:00 pm. Why does he do so? This is because he knows his wife's nature. The funny thing is that even the wife knows that if her husband has said 5:45 pm, then the train is at 6:00 pm. This means that both are aware about the deceit. Both of them are indulging in deceit. In this way, the contrast mind survives. If deceit is eliminated, what a happy life they will have!

How to be deceit free?

Imagine life when your feelings, thoughts, words and actions are synchronized. It is a life of integrity in which you feel the same as what you think, you say the same and act accordingly. It is a life where there are no more masks. Our real face is forgotten due to the mask of deceit. If you want to live as your true identity, then reduce deceit as much as possible. It may not be possible to be 100% deceit-free overnight. However, a good starting point to reduce deceit is to look at the following areas:

- Eliminate unnecessary exaggeration or hiding.
- Be truthful to yourself. Stop lying to yourself.
- Be deceit-free with your guide on the path of truth seeking.

Become deceit-free at least at one place first and taste the truth. The first relationship in which you can be deceit-free is the one between the Guru and the disciple. Then are the relationships with your spouse, children and friends. When relationships are free from deceit, there is joy and happiness in life. You can experience how blissful it would be to be truthful everywhere. Once you experience the bliss of being liberated, you would want to be deceit-free everywhere.

Initially, you might be apprehensive that this could hurt your relationships at home, at the workplace, or among friends. But soon, when the people in your life realize that you are a person of integrity, they will begin to respect you for that. They will see that you do what you say. You are honest and hence can be trusted. When the value of truthfulness and honesty reflects in your behaviour, people will trust you. If you become trustworthy, you will never be deprived of prosperity, joy, and love. Your relationships will be much better.

Henceforth, whenever the mind wants to get into deceit, you would rather say, "This is it. This is the truth. Deceit is no longer required. Life can be beautiful even without deceit." Then the contrast mind will come in the present moment and only that what is necessary will happen through the body. With continuous application of these breaks on the contrast mind, you will notice that you become more aware of what you say and get rid of the habit of compulsive lying. A strong conviction arises from within. As life becomes simple and truthful, the role of the contrast mind begins to diminish. You will experience honesty and purity in all your relationships, all your life.

Practical Exercise

Write down three examples of deceit that you have recently indulged in.

What Next?

In the next chapter, we will learn about the fourth habit of the mind.

8
Labelling

If wealth can be acquired through knowledge of the mind, so can wisdom. If prisons can be created through the efforts of the mind, so can be blissful hermitages.

Let us explore the habit of Labelling. The human mind is continuously engaged in conversation with itself. A running commentary of all that is happening around a person constantly goes on within him. Even now when you are reading, or you are at home, when you are alone or in the midst of people, the mind keeps chattering continuously, "This is good. That is bad. This should have happened. This should not have happened. This is my brother. I am a Hindu. I am a Muslim. I am a Christian. I am a woman. I am a man." The mind tries to attach different labels in every incident and creates a feeling of joy or sorrow accordingly. This happens with human beings only. Only human beings have the thinking ability. Man has the habit of attaching different labels to everything.

The impact of the habit of labelling

Let us understand how different labels are attached by different people from their own perspectives through a story. There was a heavy rain. Some people gathered under a tree waiting for the shower to stop. They started observing the tree. Did all the people have the same thoughts while observing the tree? No. All attached different labels when they thought about the tree.

In fact the word 'tree' itself is a label. However, we will use this label in order to gain more clarity on labels. The first person thought that the tree was like an umbrella due to which they got rescued from the rain. He attached the label 'umbrella' to the tree. The other person thought that the tree had superior quality wood that could be used to make a sofa. Being a carpenter, he could see a 'sofa' in the tree. He attached a label of 'sofa' to the tree. There was a herbalist who could think of the herbs of medicinal value that could be extracted from the tree. These herbs could cure diseases. The tree was a source of 'medicine' for him. There was a thief for whom the tree was a nice hideout to escape from the police. There was also a monk who could think of the tree as an excellent place for meditation.

The mind has the habit of attaching labels to everything it comes across without questioning. As soon as we attach a label, we start seeing the event or the person that way. These labels become our beliefs. They are the coloured glasses through which we see a distorted view of the world. Let us consider one more example to understand this further. Assume that you went out of your way to help your brother. Now, you are in need. If your brother does not help you, then you may get angry or disappointed. You would not be so upset if it were someone else who denied helping you. You may grumble, "He is my brother. Still, he did not help me." The label of 'brother' causes grief. If it were not for this label, one would not experience such a grief. People keep complaining, "Oh! My son did this!"; "My father did this!" These labels create miseries.

If you closely examine, the habit of labelling is one of the root causes of various negative traits of the mind such as ill-will, jealousy, hatred, greed, grief, depression, anger, worry, and boredom.

How to stop labelling?

As soon as something happens, the contrast mind immediately attaches labels and starts creating stories. Based on that, a feeling of pleasure or sorrow gets created. The contrast mind then starts looking at every incident through the same spectacle, from the same viewpoint. The mind wants to fix things and see them happening in a given way. It is uncomfortable with uncertainties when it is not sure about what is going to happen next. Because of affixing labels you consider only one side of the coin. As a result, soon the other polarity also comes to the fore. Then the duality of the contrast mind starts which gives rise to sorrow and pleasure.

When the mind is at ease with something, it labels it as 'good'. It then expects that the same should continue to happen in the future. It experiences pleasure with this label. However, if the same thing does not happen, it feels sad. If it resists something, it labels it as 'bad' and expects that it should never happen. It experiences sorrow with this label. But the reality is that life is constantly changing, there is nothing fixed. As soon as the mind gets to know that nothing is fixed, this leg of the mind starts weakening. It no longer gets into creation of stories, attaching labels. It slowly starts diminishing.

Having understood this, the next time someone says something and you start thinking, "He is trying to tell me this. However, his real motive is different." Immediately stop there and say, "This is my story, my assumption. It need not be true, isn't it? This is just a label being attached. Is that the reality?" If you go deeper and introspect, you will be amazed to find that it is never so! The other person never thinks the way we assume or imagine. We just make up our own labels and fix them, "This person is like this. He will never change." By superficial judgement, we assume, "One who does this is good", "One who does that is bad".

When we realize what exactly happens by attaching labels, how we are deviating from the truth due to this habit, then this habit will begin to diminish. In order to break the habit of labelling, tell the mind, "Do not fix anything. This is happening today. There is no need to fix that this is the way it will always happen. Change is the rule of life. Everything is constantly changing. Now it is happening this way, just accept it as it is. If it has changed then that is also fine. This is also accepted." But the mind resists change. It holds onto fixed notions, fixed labels about everything that it encounters. It tends to respond in the same predefined manner. So tell the mind, "Do not fix any response in advance. When the situation occurs, then see what response arises." With this understanding, new response will be given. Slowly, you will get free from the response arising out of old programming of the mind. You will not rely on the memory as the old response will be given by the memory. When you are open for a new response, a fresh, new response will arise from within, from the Source or Consciousness within. You will begin living in the present. As a result, you will see yourself being aware of the subtlest things around you. You will start observing everything without affixing labels. You will see them brighten with time. They will appear more colourful and livelier than before. Those things that seemed dead, which you never used to look at, will begin to reveal many secrets about them. They also have so many aspects that you never knew. You have to experience it to know that you would have never noticed such subtler aspects otherwise.

A fresh life is a label-free life

After knowing the fourth leg of the mind, if any incident happens, you will not attach any label to it. For example, you will see that someday, if you are getting bored, the mind will say, "I am feeling bored." You will immediately remember that this is the fourth leg. "I am feeling bored" is a label that you have attached. The moment you attach this label, you begin to feel bored. But if you investigate, it will immediately occur to you that this is a label. Now, you will tell the mind, "Please do not fix any label." Then you will see yourself doing something and you will be amazed how this is happening! Earlier you never did this. Earlier you used to behave like an automated machine. If you were bored, you would have started flipping through a magazine, switched through television channels, listened to music, or met up with a friend. You never realized what used to happen unconsciously.

While talking to people, you will make use of labels, but internally you will know that there are no labels. See things as they are without attaching labels. As soon as you attach a label, you will know that the fourth leg has come into action. Words such as 'engineer', 'male', 'smart', 'poor', 'happy', or 'sad' are merely stickers which can be removed. With this understanding, no event can cause sorrow.

As this habit of the mind starts breaking, you will realize that there is no duality. Success and failure, birth and death, happiness and sorrow are not different. They are polarities of the same thing. They are two sides of the same coin. If you look at things from a limited view also called as a 'well-view', this game of happiness and sorrow will continue. When you look from the 'aerial view', nothing is either right or wrong. You go beyond both happiness and sorrow.

Practical Exercise

Start observing : What do I do after attaching a label, and what do I do when a label is removed. In every event, just observe what is happening. Once the label is removed, the perspective changes. If you know that a poem is written by Shakespeare, you begin to read it with a special attention. However, when you are asked to read a poem written by your neighbour, you would read it differently. With the change in label our perspective changes. Hence, if you want to see the truth, then look at it without attaching labels.

What Next?

We have explored the four major traits of the contrast mind. By understanding and practically working within ourselves to eliminate these traits, we can train our mind for the ultimate purpose of life. The next section deals with the significance of mind training and expounds techniques to train the mind.

Part Three

Taming the Mind Training it!

9
Mission Earth

No training is required to accomplish any destructive work. Training is required when constructive work is required to be done by the mind.

Let us understand Mission Earth – the ultimate purpose of our life, the mission of our mind. After attaining Mission Earth, the mind becomes steadfast, obedient, untainted, and loving. Thereafter, transcending the mind becomes possible.

Choose a right school for the mind

Just as we choose the most appropriate and the best of the schools for our children, we should admit our mind in the best school for getting it trained.

In which of the following schools will you admit your child so as to get his mind trained?

First type of school: The level of work accomplished in this type of school is average. Activities of the intuitive mind and body discipline are taught here. With the help of this education, the child is only able to earn a livelihood in the future. Now, as parents we need to decide whether the child only needs to take care of us on completion of his education or should he be able to do something more with his life?

Second type of school: This type of school makes the child perform such exercises due to which his thinking ability opens up, and intellect develops. These children lead better lives than those trained in the first type of school.

Third type of school: Children belonging to this type of school are prepared for a higher level compared to those offered by the earlier mentioned two types of schools. In this school, you ought to be prepared for giving much more towards nurturing and developing your child. The homework of the child (mind) should be complete. The child might not want to sit in meditation. But, you ought to remind it constantly, "We have chosen a school that requires you to sit in meditation for some time." Parents too will remind themselves, "We have such high expectations from our child. Therefore, we ought to get all these done from the child." The child will create a lot of fuss. It will tell you, "Look at the other children. They all are playing. I too want to go out and play." But you need to remind it, "You have to play other games. The rules of every game are different in this school. The games that the other children are playing do not need trained body-minds. Those games can be played by anybody anywhere. They do not need any special talents. But there are some games which require trained body-minds. You have to play those games." In this way, you can convince your child that it needs to do different things. If you remain firm on your opinion, you will be successful in making the child (mind) understand.

The whole and sole purpose of the mind

After getting trained in the third type of school, the mission of our mind – Mission Earth gets accomplished. In other words, the S.O.U.L. purpose of our mind gets fulfilled. Here S.O.U.L. acronym stands for Steadfast, Obedient, Untainted, and Loving.

Let us understand this in more detail.

'S' stands for Steadfast, which means making the mind unshakable under all circumstances;

'O' for Obedient, means making the mind obedient and completely harmonized;

'U' stands for Untainted, in other words, making the mind pure by removing the filth of hatred;

'L' for Loving, implies making the mind unconditionally loving towards all.

The S.O.U.L. training of the mind is the real purpose of our life. With such a mind, our feelings, thoughts, words, and actions become congruent. Only such a mind becomes instrumental in attaining and being established in the experience of the Source.

What Next?

Having understood the whole and sole purpose of the mind, we will look at the reasons why the mind needs to be trained in the next chapter.

10
Why Train the Mind

If an impure mind acquires power, then it becomes egoistic instead of surrendering. Hence, it is essential for the mind to be clean and pure.

A man had a cat which used to trouble him a lot. The cat used to steal milk, break things in his house. So he desperately wanted to get rid of it. One day he took the cat to a remote village and left it. To his surprise, the cat returned home soon after he reached. Then he left it on the other side of the river but still it returned home. He tried one more time. He thought over a brilliant idea. He closed its eyes and dropped it very far. However, still the cat showed up the next day. After failing with so many attempts, he got frustrated. He decided to get rid of the cat forever. He took the cat to a dense forest. Thinking that the cat should not find its way back home, he went into the core of the forest. He left the cat there. This time the man himself could not find his way back home. While he was trying to escort himself out of the forest, he came across the same cat. He followed the cat and successfully reached home. Till today, he is looking out for an ultimate way to get rid of this cat.

What do we understand from this story? In this story, the cat resembles the mind. "The cat drinks milk" indicates that the mind wastes lot of our time. "The cat breaks things in the house" indicates person throws things here and there in anger. The mind is full of countless thoughts. How can one conquer over this mind and bring it under control?

Now, let us understand the ways to get liberated from the mind. You may have tried out several ways so far but which is the final solution to be tried out? The final solution could be – let the cat remain in the house and by being there it should stop troubling us. Let the cat be tied with a string of love so that it can become a cause for happiness.

From time immemorial lot of attempts were made consistently in order to master the mind. However, most of them proved to be ineffective. Although some of them could yield some results, but they were temporary. The mind calms down with these temporary remedies, but soon the old troubles and problems crop up again. How can we effectively deal with the mind? How can we train the mind? Does a wild elephant need any training to go on a rampage or to uproot any trees? No, no training is required to do that. However, an elephant needs to be trained if it needs to lift large logs of wood or blocks of stones. Training is not required to do something destructive. Training is essential when the mind is to be used to accomplish something constructive.

The demon of the untrained mind

You might have heard the story of a demon who wanted some kind of work all the time. As soon as the first job was completed, he immediately wanted another job. As per his agreement with the man, if the demon was kept free without any work then he would devour the man. Therefore, he had to be given some work all the time. Without work, the demon would kill the man whom he was serving. In order to solve this dilemma, the demon was asked to create a long ladder and was asked to climb up and down the ladder till such times that some work was given.

In this story, the demon symbolizes the mind. What work can be given to the mind so that it will remain engaged all the time? What kind of ladder is given to the mind these days? These days, people are giving the ladder of entertainment (DVDs, electronic tablets, gadgets, etc.) to the mind. You get relief from the demon of the mind for some time using such ladders. However, in the longer run, these habits prove to be detrimental. The mind likes this ladder of entertainment and tries to rewind it and play it again and again. The mind wants entertainment all the time. Without entertainment, it experiences boredom. With boredom, it gets irritated. The mind starts getting thoughts like there is no fun in life. The mind becomes a slave of moods. In this state, one does not realize that the mind is the main cause for his distress. Instead of pampering the whims of such a mind, one should consider where the mind should be engaged, what kind of ladder it should be asked to climb. A strong ladder can be formed with self-introspection and self-restraint.

Train the mind

A king brought home a monkey who kept him amused all the time with his tricks. This made the king extremely happy. One act of the monkey was particularly appealing to the king – the monkey could fan the king while he was asleep. A minister in the king's cabinet observed the monkey serving and entertaining his master. He suggested the king to impart some intermittent training to the monkey. However, the king did not see any benefit would be derived out of such training. Instead, he thought that he would get bored in the absence of the monkey. Therefore, he did not encourage this idea. Thus, the monkey was not sent for training.

One day, when the king was asleep, a fly came and sat on his nose. Seeing this, the monkey tried to ward off the fly with a sword in order to protect the king. In his attempt to do so, the monkey chopped off the king's nose.

The king represents a human being who is being served by the monkeyish mind. The mind needs to be trained so that it does not make any blunders while serving the purpose of human life. An untrained mind is like the monkey that causes damage to its master. When the mind is restless and plays mischief, it needs to be trained intermittently, so as to ensure a healthy and progressive life.

If the monkey is untrained, it will trouble the other animals staying with the king simply to prove its superiority. As a result, the king falls into the abyss of suffering. Hence, the monkey has to be trained at the right time.

Whenever you have time, invest it in training the mind. Even if you can spare half an hour, train the mind for meditation, work on its concentration, contemplate over your goal of life, perform prayers, have positive thoughts and get into selfless service. Once the mind gets trained, whatever it does will be better. After training, the mind is rid of its old wrong habits and tendencies. As soon as the mind gets trained, our body also becomes disciplined.

The school of hard knocks

Whatever incidents are happening in our life are happening in this school of Earth. The opportunities we are coming across are presented in this school itself. We are helping the mind in its training.

Everyday opportunities knock at our door. Daily incidents occur. But at that time we are ignorant that every incident is an opportunity to train our mind. Now, we need to be alert at such times and understand that it is the right time for training our mind.

In fact, every opportunity that comes into our life is part of the highest training being imparted to the mind by keeping Mission Earth in mind. We need to avail of every opportunity to make our mind steadfast, obedient, untainted, and loving. This is the right time to sow seeds. From this tender sapling, soon a magnificent tree of love, faith and happiness will grow.

What is the training in the school of life on Earth? The training is to ensure that not a single bad habit or tendency of the mind should remain. This happens by putting the mind through hard training.

If the mind gets freedom, then it will try to find its own way. If it gets everything as per its will, then it would not get ready to learn anything new.

The mind gets trained to be steadfast and progressive amidst adversities and challenges. However, we tend to keep the untrained mind in its comfort zone of pleasure, comforts, conveniences and security. We need to assess in which environment we can progress – in the midst of comfort and conveniences or amidst adversities?

This, in no way means that you need to keep away from comforts in your life. Treat comfort and conveniences as a bonus in your life that gives you relief. However, your progress will happen in the midst of those situations or in the company of those relations where you need to exercise patience. If someone says something that hurts you or if any unpleasant incident happens, then due to your old habits you react immediately. This happens because of your tendencies, habits and thinking patterns. You need to exercise patience, self-control under such circumstances. As a result, the habits of your mind will improve further.

During this training, the mind can get entangled in many things which come along the way. At such times, the mind needs to know that it is to break these tendencies that all activities are being executed on Earth. When we complete our journey along with these activities, only then Mission Earth will be accomplished.

What Next?

Having understood the need to train the mind, the next question that arises in our mind is how to train the mind. We will learn about ten different techniques to train the mind in the next few chapters.

11

Set Goals and Time Limits

*The mind is not our enemy. When efforts are made
with this understanding, it becomes easier to conquer over
the mind. We have to win over the mind not by defeating it,
but by making it victorious.*

Let us look at the first technique to train the mind. There was a leper who used to happily beg everyday sitting by the roadside. Sometimes passers by would give him alms. A man observed this beggar for some time. He thought, "What is that which inspires this man to live? What is his motivation? What is the purpose of his life? Why doesn't he think of ending his life? Every person on this Earth lives with a purpose. For some people, the driving factor could be their children. For some others, it could be to acquire more wisdom. Earning more money could be the driving factor for some people. While for some others acquiring name and fame could be the motivation in life. Everyone has a purpose to live for. What purpose does the beggar have to live?"

The man could not contain his curiosity for long. One day he asked the leper, "What is the purpose of your life? You have so many problems. You are in such a painful state. You live on this dirty road. No one cares for you. Still you are leading such a life. Why? What makes you continue with such a life?" The leper replied, "I have understood the answers to questions - Who am I really? What is the goal of my life? Why am I here on Earth? Had I not known them, I would have committed suicide a long time ago. So, whenever anyone asks me why I am living, I tell them that after seeing my true nature, the feeling of being a detached witness has awakened within me due to which I am happy. You feel that I am in grief, but I have no sorrow. I am not unhappy. Whenever a curious person like you passes by, I cry out in pain loudly so that a question should arise in you as to what makes me live despite having so much pain. I am living for you. You cannot imagine the joy I derive by performing this act."

The man was shocked to hear this reply. He never anticipated such a reply from the leper. Now, it was his turn to contemplate over the leper's reply. The leper had realized the purpose of his life. He was honestly performing his role for the attainment of this purpose.

Lord Buddha witnessed three incidents in his life. He saw an aged person. Then he saw a diseased person. After that, he came across an event of death. All these sights made him embark on the journey to seek the truth. He attained Self-realization. Did the old man or the sick man ever know that their condition would inspire someone to walk the path of truth and subsequently open a new door for the search of truth?

The leper knew the purpose of his life and hence he was living happily. There are some people on Earth whose sole aim is to cry, complain, worry, and die of hypertension or heart failure. They keep crying and complaining all through their life due to lack of clarity of their life's purpose. If only such people understand the real role they have to play in their life, then their joy knows no bounds. Their true role in life is to make people aware of stress and strain and inspire them to lead a life free from stress and strain. If this happens, then how fruitful would their life and death be? It would indeed be an exceptional service rendered by them for those suffering from stress and strain. If they realize the importance of this service to mankind, then they would play their role more effectively. After gaining an understanding, a diseased person will think, "Why should only one person change and become a Buddha? Many people can become Buddha. If this is the role I need to play in life, let this awaken in as many people as possible."

When we realize the purpose of our life, then even the greatest sorrow can become the cause of happiness. So far, we tend to be stuck in the dualities of joy and sorrow, honour and humiliation, success and failure. Assert to the mind the true purpose of the school on Earth – to train the mind. Keep reminding it of this purpose.

Set goals and time limits

After telling the mind about the true purpose of life, it is important to get support from the mind to progress in that direction. You have asked someone to do some work for you. The person agrees to do the work. You then ask him by when the job would be completed. You are looking for a job completion date by asking this question. The mind has the tendency to stretch the time to finish the task. It thinks that work can be done anytime. However, it fails to understand that by thinking in this manner and by not setting the end date, it will take indefinite time for the completion of the task. It can be a week, a month or few months or an indefinite period. There is no end to it.

The better way is to do a small amount of work every day but decide a fixed date for its completion. In this way, by setting an end date you can get the work done by the mind in a step-by-step manner. Otherwise, the mind thinks more and works less. The better way is to think less and work more.

When you set an end date to complete any work, then you commit to a deadline for finishing a job. With this, you lock the time limit for the assignment. In this way, all your tasks will get completed on time. If you want to get the work done from your mind, then you need to play this trick with the mind. You come across several opportunities when you need to work in a group. In such situations too, such habits help to get the work done in a smooth way. Whenever you assign any work to anyone, always ask for an end date for its completion. This way you help in training others' mind because everyone's mind is similar in nature. By knowing your mind, you get to know others' mind.

Setting goals that are time bound and following through on goals is one of the easiest ways of training the mind.

10 tips for training your mind through goals

1. Have goals for every area of your life – physical, mental, social, financial and spiritual.
2. Prioritize the goals – at least one most important to achieve in each area. If required, initially, take only one goal in one area
3. Pray everyday that your goals are achieved.
4. Have goals that stretch the mind. Let the goals not be too easy to achieve nor too difficult that the mind may give up.
5. Write your goals. It is essential to have the goals in writing. There is a lot of research that shows that those who had their goals in writing have successfully achieved them than those who have not.
6. Read your goals regularly. This one thing will help hugely in reinforcing the importance of being focused on your

goals.

7. Remind yourself of your true nature when you write and read your goals. When you write your goals– connect to the Source, the Consciousness within and then write. In other words, meditate for some time, be peaceful, contemplate and write your goals in a book. Do not write your goals in an agitated state. Let your goals be written from a happy natural state. In the same way, read your goals too in a happy natural state.
8. Revisit your goals from time to time.
9. Reinforce your goals based on your sensory attunement. If you are predominantly visual, create pictures of the goals both in your mind as well as in your environment. If you are predominantly auditory, create powerful sentences that reinforce your goals and post these sentences in your environment. If you are more attuned with your feelings, create a ritual every day where you re-live the feelings of what will happen when your goals are achieved.
10. Once you have written your goals, it is important to remain in a happy state. When you are happy, you become a relaxed magnet. You naturally progress towards your highest potential. When you are happy, you are in the feeling of gratitude that "It is indeed happening". Be in the feeling that whatever you have written as your goals is happening.

Practical Exercise

Set at least one goal for your mind in writing in each facet of life viz. Physical, Mental, Social, Financial, and Spiritual. Follow the checklist in the previous paragraph to see if all the points have been covered.

What Next?

In the next chapter, we will learn about the second technique to train the mind.

12

Enquire About the Mind

Contemplation is the exercise of the mind which first makes the mind pure and then helps to reach the state of no-mind. Let the mind dissolve through contemplation, not through suppression.

Let us explore the second technique to train the mind. In order to conquer over the mind, it helps to watch the mind and know its behaviour. You cannot see the wind, but you can feel its presence when leaves flutter. Likewise, if you want to see the mind, watch the thoughts. Thoughts tell you how your mind is. Instead of falling prey to your thoughts, become their master. Watch your thoughts from a neutral standpoint in a detached way.

The power of self-observation

When you watch a movie for the second or third time, you notice various details that you had not paid attention to before. In the same way, if you repeatedly keep observing your mind, you will get to know the hidden secrets of your mind. Every time you will notice newer facets of the mind. You will have newer understanding about it. Life becomes extremely easy, straightforward and peaceful for those who understand the mind. The mind can be trained through self-observation. Through self-observation, the mind realizes its reality. It understands that the root of all miseries is the mind itself and the ignorance accompanying it. The mind then becomes ready to quieten and honestly observe itself.

How to practice enquiry?

Self-observation is to watch yourself in all situations. You can practice it through an experiment. After every hour, ask yourself, "How is my mental state now?" Some common mental states are mentioned below:

1. (A – Anger) Am I getting angry on myself or on someone else?

2. (B – Boredom) Have I lost interest in working right now?

3. (C – Confusion) Am I finding it difficult to grasp something even though I have tried to do so?

4. (D – Depression) Am I depressed, worried or anxious about something for no reason?

5. (E – Ego) Do I want to be praised by someone or do I want to take credit for something?

6. (F – Fear) Am I afraid, anxious or uncertain about something?

7. (G – Guilt) Am I feeling bad and regretting something I have done or not done?

8. (H – Happy) Do I feel happy and content at this moment?

9. (I – Ill-will) Do I feel ill-will towards someone right now?

10. (J – Jealousy) Am I jealous of what other people possess at

this moment?

11. (K – Kindness) Am I feeling kind and generous towards others at this moment?

12. (L – Laziness) Am I feeling lethargic right now?

The states and desires of the mind are ever-changing. An untrained mind is restless by nature. You would notice that it is restless at one moment, and it is happy at the next moment. It is angry at one moment and greedy the next moment. It may cow down with fear at one moment and it may be anxious at the next moment. It is full of hatred and ill-will for someone at one moment, and it can be overwhelmed with the sense of guilt at the next moment. It is full of ego at one moment and filled with desires at the next moment. It can either be deceitful or logical or sensible. It may be engaged in comparison at one moment, but it may entangle itself in the web of imaginations at the next moment. It is unconscious at one moment. It is fully aware at the next moment.

In this way, if you keep watching your mind every hour, the results can be wondrous. Very soon, you will know about your mind not just intellectually, but through direct experience. You will realize that the untrained mind is illusory in nature. It cannot remain steady in one position. It is volatile and unstable.

Training the mind through enquiry

Those who practice enquiry of the mind also report that spiritual insights begin to emerge. A thought may arise: "If the mind is restless, let it be. Am I restless? Then the experience of the real 'I' – the Self – the witness of the mind will be experienced more deeply. A profound transformation can result with the understanding that the feelings of anger, ill-will, guilt, fear are all part of the mind and have nothing to do with who you truly are. An insight that practitioners of enquiry report is: "There will not be any change in my happiness due to the ever-changing nature of the mind."

Such realizations will help you attain inner and outer peace during every stressful situation in life. Just as fear is necessary for a student to prepare for his examination, in the same way, you will gain the understanding that stress is happening with the body and mind. The stress is not with you. Stress has come to get things done through the body.

With such self-observation, you will understand how you are at this point of time. This does not mean that you will know whether you are a good or a bad person, but you will know that you are now ready to do some honest self-analysis. With proper self-introspection and self-analysis, self-transformation happens automatically.

10 tips for practicing enquiry of the mind

1. If you find it difficult to practice enquiry of the mind every hour, then practice it once before you go to sleep. Look at all the actions you did during the day. You may consider beginning your day with enquiry too by examining your previous day.
2. As various aspects of the mind are revealed to you through enquiry, learn to accept whatever is revealed to you. Do not resist any aspect of the mind. Just notice the state of the mind as it is. It is important to realize that you are not undertaking this enquiry to put yourself down; but to raise your level of awareness.
3. On the same lines as the previous point, do not worry about whether the same mistake is being repeated. With consistent enquiry you will find that something from

within will alert you about your response in a given situation. Your awareness will rise. Even if the same mistake is being repeated, there is no need to be unhappy. Just continue with the enquiry and with time, repeated mistakes will also subside.

4. Be little patient with this practice. An untrained mind seeks instant results. If you are being impatient with the practice, notice that too.

5. There is no need to practice this enquiry in a seated posture. You may practice this anytime and anywhere. It is recommended that you practice it throughout the day as you go about your actions.

6. Try the enquiry of the mind immediately after major events. For example, when you get angry and shout at someone, immediately enquire at that very moment. This tremendously raises your awareness. Initially, you may find yourself becoming aware only a few hours after you became angry. With practice, you may become aware just a few moments after – or possibly even before you are about to erupt.

7. Enquire about your mind by examining your relationships. Observe yourself, i.e. the ego, in different relationships. How do you behave in front of your loved ones as compared to your subordinates at the workplace? Do you use deceit in your dealings with clients?

8. Enquire about your mind with respect to 'work' and thereby people associated with work. Ask yourself, what were your actions in different situations and what were the motives behind your actions? If you did not complete the work someone had asked you to, what was the reason? Was

it because the person who assigned you the work does not feed your ego? Or was it because he or she is a hurdle in the way of your ambitions and aspirations? If you completed the work allocated to you by someone, why did you do it? Was it because you were afraid of that person? Or was it because he satisfies your ego?

9. Ultimately, honesty is the key. Do not hide from yourself — give answers to yourself honestly. If you like someone; then what is the reason? Is it because he does whatever you ask him or is it because of his qualities? If you do not like someone, then is he really bad or is it just because he is an obstacle in your activities?

10. Remember, practice of the enquiry of the mind is different from the practice of Self-Enquiry. Enquiry of the mind helps in training it. Self-Enquiry, as a practice, helps in transcending the mind. In the practice of Self-Enquiry (not dealt with in detail in this book), one repeatedly asks the question : Who am I? In the practice of the enquiry of the mind, we are more interested in knowing how the mind keeps changing its states from time to time. The practice of enquiry of the mind does help in creating a foundation of a trained mind. A trained mind can then be transcended through Self-Enquiry or other methods.

Practical Exercise

Assess your current state by asking yourself every hour, "What is my state of mind right now?" If possible, use the A to L checklist. When you repeat this question every hour, your self-observation will turn into self-examination, and you will progress towards your inner development.

What Next?

In the next chapter, we will learn about the third technique to train the mind.

13

Concentrate the Mind

If the mind is happy and blissful, then all powers are automatically available to it and attaining Mission Earth becomes very easy.

Let us explore the third technique to train the mind. Concentration is about keeping the mind focussed on a single thing. An untrained mind does not like to concentrate. Concentration is an exercise for the mind. When the mind is engrossed in too many thoughts, then it becomes obese and gross. Such a mind is not sensitive. It cannot get into the depth of any subject. Such a mind should be made alert, sharp, subtle and sensitive. It should be trained to practice concentration.

Benefits of concentration

It is helpful to train the mind to concentrate because concentration helps to:
- Control your thoughts.
- Focus your mind.
- Be free from futile and annoying thoughts.
- Improve recollection from memory.
- Increase self-confidence.
- Raise will power.

- Take better decisions.
- Grasp and comprehend more quickly.
- Improve the ability to analyze and contemplate.
- Meditate

Concentration Exercises

To build the power of concentration, various exercises are listed below. What is common in all these exercises is that you focus consistently on only one thing.

Exercise 1: Try pronouncing your name backwards in your mind. For example, if your name is 'Monica', put the alphabets in reverse order, like 'acinoM'. In this way, try to reverse all the names you know. With complete concentration of your mind, you can achieve this. Otherwise, you will fail to do it. If you practice this every day, it will improve your power of mind concentration.

Exercise 2: Close your eyes and try to listen to the sound of a flute in your mind. There is no real flute playing in the background. Just like you playback movie songs in your mind, try to listen to the sound of a flute. Focus only on the sound of the flute and nothing else. If you hear drums or any other instrument in the background, ignore such sounds. Open your eyes after some time.

While practicing this concentration exercise, the mind may have various experiences. It may suddenly hear the flute playing one moment and the sound may stop the next moment. The flute may again start playing for some time and then stop. This happens because there is no real flute playing in the background. This exercise could be easy for someone who has very often heard the flute being played. However, it can be difficult for someone who has not heard the instrument so often or if he has not paid enough attention to it.

Continue practicing this exercise by replacing the sound of flute with the sound of other instruments like violin, guitar, drum, saxophone, trumpet, etc. As you change the instrument with every session, your power of concentration will keep improving. Try to concentrate your mind by hearing sounds of different instruments every day.

Exercise 3: Practice mental math to improve your concentration. Close your eyes and think of a two digit number with identical digits, say 44. Now think of another similar two digit number with identical digits, say 22. Now try to multiply them mentally. Remember the result in your mind. While doing this, do not apply any speed math technique. Simply do it the way you would have done it on paper, except that you are doing it mentally. Once you have the result in your mind, open your eyes and check the answer using a calculator or by doing the math on paper.

Now, attempt to multiply two non-identical two digit numbers. For example, multiply 47 by 28. You can later move to 3 digit numbers or even higher.

As you practice these exercises, you will notice that the mind is becoming single-minded. There is no other thought than what is being focused on. Single-mindedness can help in transcending the mind to reach a no-mind state.

10 tips to improve concentration

1. Concentration and interest on a topic are correlated. No wonder that those students who cannot concentrate on their studies can spend a whole day concentrating on a sport, glued to their television screens. Thus, if you want to concentrate on something and are unable to do so, then generate interest in it. To be able to concentrate better in your studies, get as curious as you can about your subjects.

This is true with work as well. Conversing with people from the chosen field helps in generating interest and thereby assists in concentration.

2. Concentration improves by focusing your mind on any single object. This could be a mantra, a picture, an object on the wall, etc. Focus on such an object to the exclusion of all other thoughts.
3. It has been observed that those who are clear about their aim are able to concentrate better. A student with goals can concentrate better than the one who does not have a clear goal. Operating under the pressure of time constraint also helps in improving concentration.
4. Concentration is also related to speed of mind. The human mind can take in 700 to 900 words per minute. Normally, we can read and understand 200 to 300 words per minute. But the mind functions at such a high speed that it can listen to about 800 words per minute. Therefore, to fill this gap, it brings about 500 words from various other thoughts. This is the reason why we find it so difficult to focus and concentrate our mind on one thing. So, what is the solution? It lies in engaging all your senses. When you are reading something, read it aloud. At the same time, try to take notes or create a synopsis of what you are reading. The more senses you involve in any activity, greater will be the concentration.
5. Vary the concentration meditations mentioned above. One day, practice one meditation. The other day, practice another.
6. Concentration also improves with contemplation. Though they are two distinct things, they are related.

Contemplation is akin to holding up a lantern to light up a room. Concentration is akin to focusing on one object with torchlight. The more you practice contemplation; the ability of the mind to hold on to one thought for a long period of time is enhanced. This in turn helps in concentration.

7. Concentration also improves with a strong intention to be a hundred percent where we are. A boy in a classroom has half his mind elsewhere. The same may be true with those at work. Thus, just cutting off all distractions and being focused on whatever you are doing helps in improving concentration immensely.

8. An anchor thought to bring the mind back is the words – "Be here now". Whenever the mind wanders away, gently tell the mind, "Be here now" and bring it back.

9. All meditation exercises do not improve concentration equally. The specific exercises mentioned above are the most useful. However, any meditation can be used to improve concentration by training the mind that wanders away during meditation. Every time the mind wanders away, bring it back to the ongoing meditation session. This simple habit can help in improving concentration.

10. One of the best meditation techniques for improving concentration is to meditate on the breath. Just focus on your breath and be aware of it. Whenever the mind wanders away from the breath, gently bring it back. This meditation, though very powerful, may be difficult for beginners. Once you have mastered the exercises mentioned above, you can graduate to this and other advanced meditation techniques.

Practical Exercise

Ensure that the mind gets a practice session of concentration on at least one of the topics mentioned above every day.

What Next?

In the next chapter, we will learn about the fourth technique to train the mind.

14

Pray and Meditate

We need to maintain a high level of consciousness through a creative outlook so that happiness is always with us and sorrow stays away forever.

Let us explore the fourth technique to train the mind. Man is troubled with the way his mind lives a double life. His mind is preoccupied with something else, and he is living a totally different life in the outside world. In order to get rid of this double life, seek help from two super powers – the power of meditation and the power of prayer. With the feelings invoked during prayer and through consistent practice of meditation, you can annihilate the roots of all your problems. You will not be touched by any problem throughout your life. You will perpetually remain in the depths of supreme silence.

Pyramid Yoga

During prayer, man puts forth some desire thought out by his intellect to God. In order to seek completion for his desires, he performs a lot of rituals. Now, we will learn a completely different type of prayer known as Pyramid Yoga which makes use of both, the head and the heart.

Following are the steps of performing Pyramid Yoga.

- Begin the prayer using your intellect. Mention your desire in words. You may utter it with your lips or repeat it in your mind.
- While breathing in say, "I am taking God inside me."
- While breathing out say, "Thank You God."
- During the inhaling process, your feeling should be as if you are letting God enter within you.
- At times, you may forget to take in God within you when you breathe in. In such a case, start your prayers again by paying full attention to what you are doing.
- Remember to utter your desire again with your lips or in mind when you resume with the prayer again. Then you can focus your attention on your breathing as mentioned earlier.

You can practice this prayer right now. Just keep this book aside for some time and do this prayer.

Pyramid yoga can be symbolically represented in the form of a triangle as follows.

Ultimate desire

Prayer   **Meditation**

Significance of Pyramid Yoga

Pyramid is a combination of two words – 'Pyra' and 'mid'. 'Pyra' stands for prayer and 'mid' stands for meditation. In short, it is the combination of both prayer and meditation.

Pyramid prayer is not an ordinary prayer. As this prayer is performed using both head and heart, it is said to be the complete way to pray.

Prayers performed with intellect raise lot of doubts and questions in the seeker's mind. With this prayer, the intellect starts becoming stable as it stops raising doubts. Even if a doubt arises, the presence of the heart quickly eradicates that doubt. Thereafter, your purpose of prayer gets fulfilled and at the same time you achieve the fruits of meditation.

As both head and heart are used during Pyramid Yoga, no doubt persists. You are simply breathing in and breathing out. When you inhale, you are taking in God. When you exhale, you express gratitude to God by saying, "Thank You!"

Generally gratitude is expressed when some wish is fulfilled, or something is achieved. However, while performing this prayer, express gratitude to God with this faith that your prayer is already fulfilled or in the process of completion. Have strong faith that your desire is bound to be fulfilled. Owing to this strong faith express gratitude to God even before your desire is fulfilled. 'Gratitude' is the shortest and the most effective prayer. As you pay gratitude in advance, your mind becomes so receptive that the desired object starts getting attracted towards you. No matter how small or big your desire is, it is bound to be fulfilled. If the mind becomes focussed, then it becomes a magnet and starts attracting the desired object. Then you attain that thing for which you have performed the prayer.

Pyramid prayer is first performed to attain worldly things. However, mere gratification of materialistic desires is not the purpose of this prayer. By performing pyramid yoga, one can obtain divine grace. With this divine grace alone transcending of the mind becomes possible. The mind becomes unshakable with grace. It then surrenders itself to attain the state of no-mind.

The frame of acceptance with the attitude of gratitude is the highest prayer of the world. Pyramid prayer can awaken the feeling of acceptance within you. Where there is a feeling of complete acceptance, the feeling of gratitude alone arises over there. When expression happens out of the feeling of acceptance, then the mind does not take any credit for it. The more the expression comes out of this feeling of acceptance, the more the mind dissolves.

Practical Exercise

Perform Pyramid Yoga as per instructions given above.

What Next?

In the next chapter, we will learn about the fifth technique to train the mind.

15

Purify the Mind

*If an impure mind acquires power, then it becomes
egoistic instead of surrendering. Hence, it is essential
for the mind to be clean and pure.*

Let us explore the fifth technique to train the mind. A man pleased God through great asceticism without purifying his mind. When asked by God about what his wish was, he sought the blessing to get whatever he wished. God granted him the wish and handed over a flower to him saying that the flower would be able to grant him whatever he wished. However, God added, his neighbour would get the double of whatever he gets. If he would get a suit, his neighbour would get two suits. Hearing this, the man felt a bit uncomfortable but agreed to the terms.

Afterwards, whatever this man asked from God, his neighbour received double of that. He asked for a television. His neighbour got two television sets. He asked for a mansion, and his neighbour received two mansions. He asked for a swimming pool. His neighbour got two swimming pools. Seeing this, his mind was filled with jealousy, malice and ill-will towards his neighbour. He was feeling miserable. When the hatred went beyond bounds, a thought occurred to his mind to harm his neighbour. Infected with this malicious thought, he asked the flower, "Blind me in one eye."

Immediately he lost one of his eyes. His neighbour too lost both his eyes and became blind. Now this person had started to lay thorns in another's path by making use of the boon he had received from God. The flower received from God could have spread fragrance to one and all. But due to the absence of purity of mind, this man began to torture himself as well as harm others.

Does this story make any sense to you? You might wonder whether someone can really go to such an extent as to harm himself. However, this is the reality of the impure mind. Man is leading such a life out of ignorance. From this example, you can see that this man could not tolerate the progress made by his neighbour due to the lack of purity of his mind. He could not properly and judiciously handle the powers given to his mind. Therefore, it is essential for man to have the purity of mind. Purity of the mind is required to handle the powers the mind attains.

A teacher has a power and a position. But if he decides to fail a student just because he caused him trouble throughout his classes in that year, then he is losing his purity of mind. The professions of teacher and doctor are noble and ideal. The nobler and higher the ideals of a profession are, greater is the need for purity of the mind. If leaders in different fields fail to have purity of mind, then their decisions will impact the masses in a big way.

The powers of the mind can help us accomplish great work. You can acquire wealth, position and fame using spiritual vitality. Hence, it is essential to work on purity of the mind to retain and control these powers. Pray for everyone's well being. Develop a feeling of unconditional love for one and all within you. By doing so, you can manage every power of the world.

How to purify the mind

The mind is ceaselessly entangled in thoughts. It constantly thinks of the past or the future. It never wants to remain in the present. Hence, our first job is to steer it from negative thoughts towards positive thoughts. You need to eliminate hatred and malice from your mind to the maximum extent possible. Learn to forgive others and practice tolerance. Purify the mind by listening to the truth, reading the truth and contemplating on the truth.

A mind that wishes well-being of others is pure and clean. If an impure mind acquires powers, then it becomes more egoistic, instead of becoming submissive. Therefore, purity of the mind is an essential requirement. Initially, you may find it difficult to fill the mind with sympathy and compassion. You will have to put in a lot of efforts to achieve this. But through consistent practice and patience, you will definitely succeed in doing this.

Every religion in the world has stressed a lot of emphasis on the need for purity of the mind. Five *Yamas* and five *Niyamas* from the *Vedic* scriptures, the five principles of peaceful co-existence known as the *Panchsheel*, the Ten Commandments have been structured to encompass the following points.

- Do not lie. Always walk on the path of truth.
- Practice non-violence. Do not kill anyone. Do not hurt anyone through your speech, thoughts, feelings or actions.
- Do not steal. Do not think of others' possessions as yours.
- Do not indulge in intoxication or other addictions like gambling.
- Do not indulge in adultery. Do not think of another man's woman as your own. Do not entangle yourself in sensual pleasures.

Brotherhood, humanity, prayers and all teachings have been formulated to calm down the mind and purify it.

Those who are living impersonal life find it easier to keep their mind pure and holy. Impersonal life is an unselfish way of living life where one is focussed on the general benefit of the masses rather than being limited by one's own personal needs. Living impersonal life means serving others selflessly, thinking of others' well-being in and through all actions.

10 tips to purify the mind

1. Be complaint free: Avoid seeing vices in others. The world appears to you as you perceive it to be. The world will appear to be of the same colour as that of the spectacles you wear over your eyes. Remind yourself that the fault lies in the very thought that there is a fault in others.
2. Ask for forgiveness: Asking others for forgiveness for having hurt them helps in increasing purity. If you lack the courage to speak directly and ask for forgiveness, at minimum, ask for forgiveness mentally. Even this will help as far as purity is concerned.
3. Forgive others: If you are holding a grudge against someone for something they did to you or your family, forgive them mentally. Forgive others for your own benefit.
4. Forgive yourself: If you are having any guilt about what you have done in the past or failed to do in the past, forgive yourself. This will help in purifying the mind.
5. Open your heart and pray: Every night, open your heart and pray for others. Keep good thoughts for others. Again when you get up in the morning, open your heart and spread love. The best way to open your heart is through prayer. Pray for the whole world. Visualize white light from

top of the Earth and golden light arising from bottom of the Earth. White light represents purity and golden light represents Consciousness. Praying is the best way for opening the heart. This immensely helps in increasing purity.

6. Keep your ideal in front of you: Be inspired by someone who is the epitome of purity. This can be your Guru or someone you know. Keep that ideal in front of you. Whole day, think about that ideal. Focus on that ideal and purity shall increase.
7. Be in the attitude of gratitude: The feeling of gratitude also improves purity. Be thankful for everyone in your life and all the good things in your life. Express gratitude directly.
8. Train your eyes to be pure: A key way to be pure is by training your eyes. Avoid lustful fantasizing, aimless surfing of programs on television, watching movies without any limit or restraint, trash and worthless stories in daily publications, etc.
9. Train your speech to be pure: Training your speech also helps in purity. Avoid uttering harsh, rude, bad or abusive language. Avoid sarcasm or scorn even if it is in response to someone speaking harshly to you. Avoid backbiting, rumour mongering, use of abusive words completely. Be in training your eyes or your speech, what you are actually training is your thoughts. In the same vein, be careful of what you are hearing. Even though you may be practicing pure speech, it is important to be in the company of those who see, speak and act purely.
10. Train your actions and body to be pure: Let all your actions reflect purity. Avoiding acts of deceit and being committed

to the work you are doing will help in making your actions and thereby your mind pure. The body and mind are interconnected. A clean body will automatically help in keeping the mind clean and pure too.

Practical Exercise

Every night before going to sleep go through your dealings with people during the day without bias. Wholeheartedly with complete purity of mind, perform following prayer.

I forgive all who have hurt me knowingly or unknowingly today.
By doing this, I am not doing favour on anyone, but myself.
I am increasing my level of purity of mind.
I am raising my level of Consciousness.
I am bringing joy and prosperity in my life.
Today whomever I have hurt with my feelings, speech and actions I seek forgiveness to them by making God a witness.
Please forgive me. I will not commit this mistake again.

What Next?

In the next chapter, we will learn about the sixth technique to train the mind.

16
Employ the Mind in Selfless Service

The mind needs to be trained to cultivate selfless feelings so that it aids in attaining our goal rather than being an obstacle.

Let us explore the sixth technique to train the mind. The mind entertains both positive as well as negative thoughts. While we benefit from positive thoughts, we suffer the ill-effects of our negative thoughts. The natural tendency of the mind is to get attracted towards negative thoughts. The mind gets contaminated with negative thoughts. The goal is to make this mind steadfast and pure. Therefore, the need is to engage the mind into selfless service so that the mind can become pure.

Let the mind become a tool and not a hindrance to achieve your goal. For this, you need to train your mind to cultivate impersonal feelings. Initially the mind will not agree to this, but it is your responsibility to make it agree. The mind will say, "I don't need to do selfless service." But you know that the mind will think positively only by getting into selfless service. You need to convince the mind that selfless service is extremely essential for its wellbeing.

With selfless service, the mind will get immersed in service and devotion. It does not matter whether the service is trivial or significant. The mind will engage into everything with the feeling of service. Such a mind is ever prepared to render service on time wherever needed.

When the mind serves selflessly, it can finish a job in a month which would have otherwise taken six months. This is because now it has a great cause, a grand purpose, a powerful goal to work for. The real purpose is to purify the mind of impurities. Sometimes some tasks may seem to be impossible to complete as per the agreed time. However, if we determine to complete them before time, then they do get completed. We must resolve to finish all our tasks before time. Then we will see them getting completed on time.

Time is an aspect of the mind. Depending on the state of the mind, time may appear to be long or short. When the mind is not comfortable with performing a task, it appears to drag on for a longer period of time. However, when the mind is absorbed in something very interesting, then time appears to fly by very fast. In the same way, when the mind experiences the joy of selfless service, it goes beyond time. Hence, always engage the mind in selfless service.

Prepare the mind for an impersonal life

All the activities that are happening on Earth are all impersonal in nature. Nothing is personal. It is just like a machine that has many parts. All the parts work in a co-ordinated and orchestrated manner for the same machine. No part of the machine works in isolation. In the same manner, all people in the world too are a part of the Consciousness, the Source. However, the feeling of a separate 'I' (the ego) is born in man due to the contrast mind. As a result, he looks at everything from an individualistic perspective.

But when man attains higher understanding, he realizes that all activities in the world are impersonal in nature. Then why did the mind come into existence at all? This is because even the entry of the mind is as per the grand divine plan. The mind had to come.

It is due to this mind that true knowledge can be grasped. Had the mind not been there, all activities on Earth would have ceased to exist. It is owing to the mind that man can discriminate between truth and untruth. He can understand the difference between them and think over it. The experience of truth is possible only when the mind is made instrumental towards that purpose.

A magician had some goats. He used to slay one goat every day. He had hypnotized all the goats to make them believe that they were actually lions. Every day he used to slay one goat in front of all other goats. Because they were hypnotized, none of them ever realized that their turn too would come one day. Every goat had only one thought in its mind, "I am the lion. The others are all goats. Hence they are being slain."

The same game is being played with the mind. It has assumed a separate identity and individual existence for itself and hence it is under some misconceptions. These misconceptions become stronger with time due to ignorance and the way upbringing happens. Whatever is happening around also helps to strengthen these misconceptions. If you carefully observe the manner in which individuals speak at large, you will realize that they believe themselves to be doers and lead a highly personal and constricted life. They lead life by carrying a burden. When man functions with the feeling of doer-ship by believing himself to be the doer, then all work accomplished by him becomes personal. Man has completely forgotten that he is part of the same divinity, the Consciousness, the Source. Once he realizes this, his mind will immerse itself in selfless service.

Practical Exercise

Consider all yours tasks impersonal and try to finish them before time for a day.

What Next?

In the next chapter, we will learn about the seventh technique to train the mind.

17

Energize the Mind

The mind should have the understanding: "Every incident in our life is coming as an opportunity." Only when the mind recognizes every incident as an opportunity, it will be able to derive happiness from every incident.

Let us explore the seventh technique to train the mind. Everyone knows that our body has an effect on the mind. When the body is ill, the mind gets irritated even with the most trivial of matters and troubles us. Likewise, the health of the mind too affects the body. Hence, it is imperative to understand both, the body and the mind, to keep the body healthy. The tongue (food intake) needs to be brought under control in order to make the body healthy. To attain good mental health, one must exercise control on the mind.

The interdependence of body-mind

The mind and the body share a mutually dependent relationship and affect each other profoundly. Hence when the mind begins to listen to us, staying healthy becomes easy for us. You will become the master of your body and mind, and not the other way round.

When your eyes will see only that which you ought to see, the imagination faculty of the mind will come under control. When your ears will hear only that which you ought to hear, you will then attain spiritual health. When your tongue will eat only that which you ought to eat, you will then attain good physical health. When your tongue will speak only that which you ought to speak, you will have healthy relationships. When your skin will experience only that what you ought to experience, then you will experience the eternal bliss (the essence of Consciousness). When your mind will think only that what you ought to think, you will then attain mental health.

It would not be wrong to say, "Your health is under the control of your mind." Those who always harbour thoughts of hatred, ill-will and malice in their mind invite many illnesses of the stomach and the heart. Many a times, a heart attack is usually a hate attack or an attack of negative thoughts. The attack of negative thoughts implies the attack of worry and depression. A mind filled with worry can even drive a man to insanity. The poison of worry begins to spread gradually and makes man a storehouse of illnesses.

Negative thoughts drain the mind of all enthusiasm and positive energy due to which man becomes distressed and depressed. Such a person no longer wants to live. By giving up the desire to live, he takes very long to become healthy. The one, who has a strong desire to live, attains good health rapidly. The one, who has got the goal to attain Mission Earth, has got a lot of challenging work to do. His mind is filled with creative and constructive thoughts and a strong will to live. Such people fight the biggest of diseases and come out well with victory. Always keep hope alive in your mind. Always keep your primary goal in front of your eyes. Keep reminding yourself continuously about it until you are completely absorbed in it.

When you eat, remind yourself, "I am eating this food in order to attain my goal. This will make my body healthy, and my body will fully support me to attain my goal." Such kind of thinking will not let you over-eat even by mistake. You will always have control over your tongue and will not give in to its craving for tasty food and drinks. You will always have a proper diet. You will perform necessary physical exercises and will take proper rest.

A mind filled with anger and stress creates tension in one's nerves that manifests as pain. This stress can extend from three hours up to three days. When you welcome the feeling of acceptance in your mind, this stress immediately begins to diminish and dissolves. Otherwise, one may even resort to taking sleeping pills for an extended period of time. You may take medicines depending on your need, but it is critical to eliminate the root cause of stress.

By entertaining the thoughts of fear and doubt, your inner strength weakens. Thoughts of fear are the biggest enemy of your self-confidence. It is only due to fear and doubt man is not able to do what he is supposed to do on Earth. The fear – "What will people say?" – deprives man from attaining Mission Earth.

Just as there are various illnesses that affect the body, the mind too suffers from illnesses such as anger, ego, fear, worry, hatred, ill-will, jealousy, stress and greed. Man suffers from indigestion due to these illnesses. If one tries to hide any of these vices of the mind from others, it causes harm to him. Ego, deceit, hatred and such other vices of the mind create diseases of the stomach.

It has been observed that people who are troubled with negative thoughts do not feel like giving anything to others. They have trouble in clearing their bowels due to this miserly habit. Additionally, their skin does not sweat easily and their lungs have trouble in exhaling completely.

Recovery of your health

In your daily routine, never say anything negative involving any part of your body. For example:
- "This person is such a headache." Those who keep saying this are often victims of headaches.
- "Looking at him makes my blood boil." People who say this have been observed ending up with high blood pressure and hypertension.
- "He really gets up my nose." This complaint often leads to breathing problems.
- "I don't want to see my neighbour. He is a thorn in my eye." People who use such expressions could suddenly begin to turn blind or fall prey to some disease related to the eyes.
- "This job is a noose around my neck." People who say such words are seen to have some neck and shoulder problems.

Try to find out the cause of your ailments. Find out whether these ailments are due to wrong eating habits, improper sleep habits or lack of exercise. If you do not have any wrong habits, then introspect with a calm mind the thoughts you are entertaining that could have caused this illness. When the cause of your illness is not detected at the physical level, it is certain that the illness is caused due to the impurity in your thoughts.

Rather than entertaining negative thoughts, you can take care of your health through positive thoughts to a large extent. You need to find out the reason for your stress on time and accept it. It is entirely in your hands to bring stress under control on time. You need not expect it from others. You should not feel depressed even on being insulted. Negative thoughts invite ailments which the body has to endure in a longer run. Therefore, adopt the policy of having only positive thoughts without encouraging any negative thoughts. In order to get away from the illnesses caused by thoughts, guide these thoughts in an appropriate direction and boost their power. Enhance your health through auto-suggestions.

Towards the positive mind

Repeating a thought several times aloud or in the mind is called self-suggestion. Along with the treatment you are taking for your illness, use the power of the mind as medicine by repeating the following self-suggestions with love and complete faith.

- ✓ The disease which is no longer required in my body is now leaving my body.
- ✓ All the necessary hormones and enzymes required for good health are getting created in my body.
- ✓ I always feel young and enthusiastic.
- ✓ I am getting better and better. I am feeling completely healthy.
- ✓ If at all there is any illness in my mind or body, it is quickly getting cured.
- ✓ Every day in every way at every moment, my body is getting better and better.
- ✓ Every day in every way in every part, I am getting better and better.
- ✓ I am God's property. No illness can harm me.

Every day, as often as you can, tell this to yourself, "I am magnificent. I never fall from magnificence. To be troubled is nothing but a fall from that magnificence which is not in my nature. I have stopped getting troubled. Everything that happens in my life happens according to the divine plan. The endless grace of the divine power is guiding me at every stage of my life."

Visualize that you are undergoing the process of recovery from illness. You are experiencing the feeling of becoming healthy again. Whenever you feel the need, repeat these happy thoughts, "I am getting free of my negative thoughts, and I am at peace with myself. I have faith in life, and I am secure. I am experiencing happiness arising out of my habit of thinking positive thoughts. I am peaceful, important and complete. I love and accept myself. I deserve to be loved. I am feeling fresh. I lovingly take care of my body, brain and all other parts of my body. I express the joy of life and accept it. I am confident that always all the right things are happening in my life. I am Consciousness. I am flowing with every experience of life in great joy. Everything is going on smoothly. I am happily freeing myself of the past and I am now at ease. I now live in the present. My life is overflowing with happiness. Thoughts of joy and bliss are now easily flowing through me."

When you repeat a thought again and again, it enters your inner mind or subconscious mind. This is called programming of the mind. This programming can be both negative as well as positive. Therefore, harbour thoughts such as : "I have abundant money. I have abundance of self-confidence. I can accomplish every task with the help of God." Always keep your mind occupied fully with positive, happy thoughts. Never repeat any of the above-listed negative thoughts or anything that resembles them. Whenever such thoughts arise, or you are about to speak such words, change them immediately. In this manner, begin to enrich your mental health and very soon you will see its effects on your physical health.

Just as a mother neatly arranges all the toys that her child has strewn around when the child falls asleep, so does your inner mind neatly arranges the thoughts that you harbour while you sleep at night. Therefore, always inspire yourself with positive thoughts before you go to sleep at night. Every night before you go to bed always do prayer and give self-suggestions for complete health. Never give up the hope to live. Always have the feeling of acceptance, happy thoughts and self-suggestions. Your mind will always remain happy and healthy with this.

When you consistently use the power of self-suggestions through their repetition, you can walk on the path of truth fearlessly, breaking all your patterns, tendencies and bad habits. When you are able to do so, you will attain great mental health and feel abundance of happiness.

Practical Exercise

Choose one or two inspiring self-suggestions from those listed earlier. Every day write them down ten to twenty times in a diary and read them aloud. Prepare a rhythm and a tune to repeat them. Keep humming them happily and allow your brain to keep thinking on these inspiring self-suggestions throughout the day. Self-suggestions that are repeated constantly soon turn into reality. This method is very effective in keeping the mind healthy at all times.

What Next?

In the next chapter, we will learn about the eighth technique to train the mind.

18

Safeguard the Mind

An aspiration to live, a feeling of acceptance, happy thoughts and self-suggestions always keep the mind healthy and contented.

Let us explore the eighth technique to train the mind. Avoiding bad company is essential to gain victory over the mind. Bad company does not just mean the company of drunkards, drug addicts, gamblers or criminals alone. It also includes the company of those things which have a bad impact on you. Knowingly or unknowingly you develop interest in bad things. This gives rise to negative thoughts within you and some beliefs take root within you. They have a bad influence on the mind. If you see someone's death, thoughts of death may begin in your mind. You may begin to think, "It is the bitter truth of life that everyone has to die some day. So how should we live from now onwards?" You are bound to get influenced by whatever you come in contact with. Hence, you need to be very conscious and careful about the company you keep and the topics you discuss.

Avoid bad company

An incident occurs. If the mind gets attached to it, then various thoughts related to the incident emerge within you. If these thoughts take you away from the present moment and change your state of mind, then it is a bad company. Therefore, whenever you come in contact with anything or any incident, contemplate whether that company is good or bad.

If someone hurts your ego, you feel humiliated. In such a situation, you come in contact with your ego, which is a bad company. You need to reflect on this bad company. Association with the ego makes the mind impure and gross. Such a mind always likes to get engaged in arguments and cultivates hatred.

Save your mind from seeing vices in others. By seeing vices in others, you indirectly get in contact with them. This is also a bad company. Watching your own faults is not a bad company.

Watching the television, reading newspaper is also a kind of company because thoughts emerge within you through such contacts. Do not get too much addicted to these as it will hamper your planned activities and in turn you will get deviated from your goal.

Impact of bad company

One cannot claim that bad company has no effect on him. Bad company cannot affect us only if the mind is filled with divine devotion and love for the truth. Otherwise, people who make such claims end up becoming exactly like those in whose company they are. For example, a person who accompanies his friend for alcohol finds himself habitual to the habit of drinking alcohol when he is in distress. This is the influence of bad company. Hence, we should never make such claims and always stay away from harmful company.

The world appears to you as you perceive it to be. The world will appear to be of the same colour as that of the spectacles you wear. If you wear red glasses on your eyes, the world will appear red to you. This implies that man gets influenced by every incident and every person he comes in contact with.

The intellect becomes corrupted due to bad company. Even during such times, if your mind is filled with divine devotion and love for the truth, then despite being in bad company you will not get stuck in it.

Open your intellect

If you wish to achieve victory over the mind, save the intellect from being corrupted and avoid bad company. If the intellect is lost, man ends up harming himself. The intellect and the power of discrimination are the only tools that help you in the attainment of Mission Earth.

Open your intellect by investigating on the following guidelines.

- Ask yourself, what are the things you come in contact with, what are the things you get associated with. Then reflect on them.
- In order to understand Mission Earth and recognize the opportunity, investigate : What is the purpose of your life? What is the whole and sole purpose of human life? What is Mission Earth?
- If the mind tries to deviate from the goal of Mission Earth, ask these questions to your intellect : Which direction do you want to go and why? Why is it necessary? Till today who all have traversed the path of winning over the mind? What did they say? By treading this path, did they truly attain happiness or did they repent over their decision?
- When you are in misery, investigate : Who am I? What is the reason for my sorrow? When and why does sorrow occur? Is it that the creator of sorrow is residing within us? Why do we search outside for the cause of our sorrow?

When your intellect opens up and blossoms, the question, "Who am I?" will arise. Then you will be able to grasp many subtle aspects about yourself. For example, when you take a pen in your hand, do you ask, "Who is this?" No, you do not because you know that it is a pen. The very fact that the question, "Who am I?" has arisen implies that you are not the body. If you were the body, then this question would not have arisen at all. When you say, "I thought about this thing," or "I brought in this thought," it implies that "I am not the mind; I am the one who brought this mind. I am the witness, the seer of the mind." When such questions arise in the intellect, the power of discrimination awakens. Then you will start differentiating between the truth and the un-truth. The understanding of what exactly the truth and the untruth are will emerge within you.

Opening up of the intellect becomes easy when you are constantly in touch with that which is ever awake. If you come in contact with that, then your life will get transformed. The onset of a living master where Self-realization has taken place serves as a wonderful arrangement for the intellect to open up. It then becomes easier to win over the mind.

What company should you engage the mind in?

You should engage your mind in the following associations of people.

Good company – Be in the company of people who are good, virtuous and well wishers of all. By being in this company, you realize that the ill effects that could have happened on your mind due to bad company do not occur.

Bright company – In this company, you get in touch with people who have begun to walk the path of truth. Experientially they have begun to know the answer to "Who am I?" They may be hyperactive or lethargic in nature, but at least the love for truth has arisen within them. Whenever they speak, they will speak only about the truth. They are truth lovers. They never feel tired of speaking about the truth. As a result, being in their company your divine devotion is bound to rise. This opens up the possibility of having a pure, unshakable and loving mind.

Company of bright truth – This is the company of a Guru. In this company, you are guided on the path of Self-realization and Self-stabilization. Your mind becomes unshaken and you start living in the state of perpetual peace and joy.

Practical Exercise

Contemplate on the things, people you come in contact with and their impact on you. Avoid bad company as far as possible.

What Next?

In the next chapter, we will learn about the ninth technique to train the mind.

19

Move Your Mind

When mental stress gets associated with the physical stress, tension is the result. Mind is the actual cause for tension.

Let us explore the ninth technique to train the mind. When there is mental stress, it affects the body in the form of physical stress. The mental stress is associated with the mind, whereas the physical stress is associated with the body. When mental stress gets associated with the body, physical stress begins to develop. The true reason of physical stress is mental stress. When there is physical stress, affirm to yourself, "This stress is worthwhile. It has come to get some work done." Because of this stress, some work will get accomplished.

Stress is also associated with the intellect. When the intellect opens up, awakening of Self happens. Then one will come to know how to make use of the physical stress. When Lord Buddha saw both an old man and a diseased person, he got mental stress along with physical stress. He got worried, "Will this happen to me too? Will the same thing happen with my mind and body too?" Then he saw death from close quarters and last of all, he saw the life of a monk. Seeing the death of a person, he realized that the tension in that body got over with the death, but that was of no use to that person because there was no life force left over there. There was no movement. Only passivity was left in that body. No movement was possible with that body. It was a corpse.

When there is a balance between hyperactivity and passivity in a person, then equanimity gets developed. In addition to the dead body, Lord Buddha also saw a monk who was balanced. Thus, looking at both the scenes of hyperactivity and passivity, he got intellectual stress. That was the beginning of his journey for Self-realization. The intellect and the power of discrimination were awakened. He started reflecting on how to search the truth, what the goal of life was and how to get rid of the mental stress and sorrow. In the beginning, Lord Buddha could only see sorrow and physical stress all around. Then he set out in search of the right path to find the remedy for this.

In order to get rid of physical stress, work upon your mental stress. You need to start with intellectual understanding for that. It is the understanding, the experience, the attribute-less state in which you are fully convinced that stress has come to the body, and not you. In order to arrive at such a state, you need to attain the state of equanimity. Opportunities are knocking on your door every day in your life. Incidents are happening. Every day you are going through some stress. But you need to see to it that it remains only a physical stress and does not turn into mental stress.

You need to develop the thinking that every incident is coming in your life in the form of an opportunity. When you will start looking at every incident as an opportunity, then you will derive happiness from it. Incidents in your life are helping you to attain the highest goal of your life. If you always remember this understanding, then you will be able to give the right response in every incident despite having physical stress. You will have a smile on your face all the time. Otherwise, in stressful situations you will say, "How will this happen? In such a situation, how can I smile? What will people say?" If you are not able to smile in front of people, you could at least enjoy from within.

Body and mind are deeply associated with each other. The physical stress affects the mind due to which the mind experiences the feeling of hopelessness. The mental stress in turn has an effect on the body. The body experiences fatigue, exhaustion and weakness. Those who understood this phenomenon came up with a formula of controlling the body in order to control the mind. According to this formula, in the midst of stressful situations if you do not lose patience and courage at the physical level, then very soon the mental stress too will disappear.

This formula not only helps you get rid of physical stress, but you derive happiness, confidence, courage and health using this formula. Understand this through an example. Suppose you are about to step into situations like performing on the stage, going for an interview, or going for an examination and you begin to feel fear, lack of confidence, inferiority complex and nervousness. Then act as if you are being awarded the prize for the best actor and you are going to receive it on the stage. Act as if you are not experiencing any physical stress. If you think on these lines, then you will get into action with elegance. You will walk with your chest forward and head held high. With this action of the body, self-confidence will begin to build up in your mind. You will feel free of physical stress, mental stress and will be full of courage. You will be surprised how you can be rid of mental stress and begin to feel confident merely by acting.

Till today people have been committing a common mistake. They think, "When we will experience self-confidence, then we will walk absolutely upright. When we are not under stress, we will smile and be happy." But you need to understand this formula of mind Science which says, "Our feelings change as per the actions (acting) of our body." On understanding this formula, you will not wait for stress or fear to recede. But with your body you will act as if you are calm, relaxed and brave in the situation. This acting will generate a new energy in your body. If you work according to this formula, self-confidence will grow in you and you will begin to feel free from stress.

Wherever you are sitting right now, observe yourself how you are seated. If you feel that you are sitting in a wrong posture (stooped, constricted), then immediately open up and sit straight. Be seated in such a way as if you are ready to face any situation. Open both your hands and feel within yourself how the joy of self-confidence is; how it is to be free from mental stress. In this manner, observe yourself while walking, speaking and performing activities. Whenever you find yourself stressed, fearful and constricted, apply the above formula and change your body language to that of a courageous person. Act as if you are a prince who is relaxed and content. In this manner, you can get free from mental stress by deliberately changing your body language and actions.

Why cannot people start with any work? They think that they should first feel the urge from within to do that work. Until they get such a drive from within, they cannot begin that work. It is worth reflecting on whether action follows the feeling or vice versa. In reality, action and feelings go together. By changing your feelings your action changes and by changing your actions your feelings change. By controlling your actions, you can also control your feelings. This implies that interest can be aroused if you carry out a seemingly boring task with enthusiasm. To act this out is easier because actions are directly under the control of the desire, whereas feelings and interest or mood are not directly under your control. By understanding this formula, do not keep waiting for interest or mood or feeling to awaken, instead get on with the job. Do everything with the feeling as if you love doing that work. Use your will power completely. By knowing this formula, you will become unshaken and free from physical and mental stress forever.

Practical Exercise

For every stressful situation you undergo during the day, affirm to yourself, "This stress is worthwhile. It has come to get some work done."

What Next?

In the next chapter, we will learn about the tenth, the last technique to train the mind.

20
Engage Your Mind in Creativity

The one, who has resolved to attain Mission Earth, has a powerful goal to accomplish. His mind is filled with creative and constructive thoughts. He has a strong will to live life. He is able to recover and come out of even grave illnesses.

Let us explore the tenth, the last technique to train the mind. Mind is the creation of God and hence the mind too can create things. The mind experiences joy when it expresses the creative quality of God. On experiencing joy, the creative mind keeps itself away from the tendency to destroy. Hence, teach the mind the art of being creative. Whenever the creative mind sees something, it immediately foresees the future possibilities of that thing. It recognizes how that thing is going to form up in the future.

See 'New' in everything

People consider something as 'new' if it has just come out of a manufacturing unit. But this is not true. If something is newly painted with a colour, it does not mean that it has become new. Lot of things need to be added to it in order to make it complete. When all the possibilities related to that thing are opened up, it will become a new thing. Look at the old cars and the new cars. Which cars would you call as 'new'? The old car is not of much use, and the new car is highly effective. That means all the possibilities of the new car have got opened up. Had you shown an old car to a creative person in the past, he would have foreseen a lot of new possibilities in that car. He would have suggested that many things still need to be added to that car. The mind too should attain such a creative foresight. As a result, man should be able to see the new and the complete set of possibilities in every incident, every object and every action.

When you see a table in your home, ask yourself, "Is this table old or new?" If you see many possibilities can be opened up in it, then you need to understand that the table is old. Even though it is bought new from the furniture shop, many things can still be added to it to make it 'new' in the future. Actually, let all the possibilities in that object be explored, and it should become what it can become in the future. How will the pen be in the future? How will the car be in the future? How will the table be in the future? A creative mind can see all these possibilities. Train your mind to see how things that are currently in progress will become in the future once they are complete.

A man needs to scold people to get the work done at his workplace. Now if he thinks, "What new experiment should I conduct in such a troublesome environment? If at all I have to scold people, then why not do it in different ways every day?" If he conducts these experiments, then will the scolding be a trouble for him anymore? It will not. In fact by doing this, he will be able to accomplish his work as well as properly guide his anger with awareness. The energy that was used to express anger will now be directed towards creative work.

Become a possibility thinker

All over the world people either harbour positive thoughts or negative thoughts. But very few people harbour creative thoughts. Creative thinking comes as a next step to positive thinking. It is a great boon in itself. Give space to creative thinking in your life. Understand this with an example which elaborates what a new and creative thought would be. Whenever an incident occurs in your life, how do you look at it? Do you look at it from the perspective of a positive thinker, a negative thinker or a possibility thinker? A possibility (creative) thinker makes use of the intuitive mind.

A mother had three sons. One day she gave a bottle to her eldest son and asked him to buy oil from a shop. The son bought oil. While he was returning home, he fell along with the bottle. Half of the oil spilled out from the bottle. He came home crying and narrated to his mother how half the oil spilled out and was wasted. This boy was a negative thinker who always saw the negative side of things. He was unhappy and always remained unhappy.

The elder son was a positive thinker. He too was sent by his mother to the market to bring home a bottle of oil. The same incident happened with him too, and half the oil spilled out. But he came home laughing and narrated to his mother how half the oil was saved even when the bottle fell on the ground. This boy gave importance to positive thinking and always remained happy with this thinking.

The youngest son knew how to always think about future possibilities. He was a possibility thinker. After every incident, he focussed more on what could be done immediately after the incident and in the future. The same incident took place with him, but he told his mother, "Such and such incident occurred. Half of the oil is intact, half spilled out. But I will come home a bit late today. I will work somewhere to earn some money so as to cover up for the loss that we incurred." He could think of the future possibilities. The youngest son first thought of the positive aspect of the event. At the same time, he did not ignore the negative aspect. Moreover, he thought positive to make up for the loss incurred in the process. He was at poise while making up for the loss. He became alert about how not to repeat the same mistake again and constantly treaded the path of progress to a happy and successful life. Your mind should also become a possibility and creative thinker like the youngest son.

Train your mind to develop creative outlook

What price have you paid for whatever you have attained so far in your life? By any chance have you paid a bit too high price? If you have paid a greater price, then do not do the same in future. Otherwise, whenever negative events take place, you become unhappy and end up paying a greater price emotionally in the form of sorrow. When someone called you a fool or an ass or abused you, you spent hours or even days brooding over it. Is it right being agonised by that incident for so many days? To pay such a price is a costly bargain. From today itself embrace new thinking. Make your mind creative and lead a happy life.

Is it easy to become creative? Yes! It is easy when the mind is not headstrong, and the intellect is flexible. A flexible intellect can see any event, object, aspect or subject with a new perspective. One day a person asked Lord Mahavira, "Is it good or bad to sleep for long hours?" The answer that Lord Mahavira gave demonstrates a new perspective. He said, "It is good for a bad person to sleep for long hours since he will no longer spread violence in the society. He will remain free from violence for some time. However, if a good person sleeps for a short duration, it is good. The longer he stays awake, the more he will spread the lesson of non-violence and love in the society."

When a piece of land is seen from different angles, different sights are revealed. But, when the same piece of land is seen from a helicopter (from above), the whole truth about that land becomes visible. This is only an example to illustrate the vital importance of developing a creative outlook.

If by looking at something a negative thought occurs to the mind, "I will not be able to buy this thing." At that time, learn to quickly change your thought and ask yourself, "How can I buy this thing?" Then start thinking on this question. By thinking in this manner, positive and creative thoughts will begin to flow in your mind.

You need to raise your level of consciousness by having creative outlook and creative thinking. By doing this, you will always remain happy, and unhappiness will stay away from you. To make all this possible, bring creative thinking into practice. Let creative thinking seep into your daily life and take its appropriate place in your mind. Give space to creative thinking in your life. Let it be the chief part of your daily activities. In this way, by getting engaged into creative endeavour, you will be able to guide your mind in a right direction. This will not only benefit you, but the world will also benefit from it.

Practical Exercise

Today while performing activities throughout the day, wherever you get a thought "I cannot do it", ask yourself "How can I do it?" By thinking in this manner, positive and creative thoughts will begin to flow in your mind.

What Next?

In the next part, we will learn about how to go beyond the mind, how the mind can become a cause for supreme happiness, and some questions and answers about the mind.

Part Four

**Beyond the Mind
Transcending it!**

21
Transcending the Mind

*Pull out the mind from its habit of thinking in extremes.
Thinking in extremes is an old habit of the mind. Hence, you
need to first see the bad habits of the mind, so that its
habit of running into the extremes is stopped.*

By now you would have realized that the only reason for all your problems is your mind. However, the same mind can become the reason for great happiness in the longer run. Let us understand how to slim this mind in order to transcend it.

When one is not skilled enough to make use of a knife, he often ends up cutting his fingers. But as soon as he becomes proficient in its proper usage, he finely cuts vegetables with the same knife, more efficiently than before, without injuring his fingers. The same is true with the mind. After the mind is admitted to the gym of the mind, it becomes instrumental in creating joy, love and peace in our life.

Admit the mind to the gym of the mind

If someone has grown fat, he gets reminders from everyone to slim down. Then, he joins a gym to make his body slim and trim. He is asked to go through physical exercises in the gym to lose his extra weight. Initially, his hands begin to tremble, his legs get itching sensation. But with regular practice, he gets over these problems. His stamina increases and he gets ready to take up more exercises.

The same is true with our mind as well. But, our mind being invisible, we do not get reminders from anyone to make our bulky mind slim. As a result, no work is done on it. But, in order to attain Mission Earth, we need to admit our mind in the gym of the mind. Just like the gym for the body, the gym for the mind also has different exercises to strengthen the mind. As we go through different incidents in our life, the mind looks at each of them from an old viewpoint. As a result, it becomes happy or sad. After admitting the mind in this gym, right understanding is imparted to the mind to train the thoughts, observe patience and give a response filled with devotion and right behaviour. With this, the mind becomes steadfast, obedient, untainted and loving. Such a slim mind then remains in the state of surrender to the Consciousness, the Source. Transcending the mind then becomes easy.

Exercises in the gym of the mind

When the mind troubles you and becomes unhappy, ask yourself, "How am I looking at this incident?" The very fact that you are feeling troubled proves that you are looking at the incident from a wrong perspective, or there are wrong thoughts going on in your mind. The mind paints a picture of thoughts and says, "What is going on is very bad. Why is this happening to me alone? What will be my future? Will I continue to live like this?" You assume the thoughts of your mind to be a reality. You believe, "Things will always continue in this manner, and I will never get any value or respect from anyone." When the mind says all such things, you are looking at the incident from a negative perspective. You do not realize that whatever is happening in your life is the outcome of your own prayers.

You always wished to have the highest achievements. Therefore, you have prayed, "I should get a good job which will help me create new things." Now, as a result of your prayer, some situations are created. However, your body is not trained for that. Your eyes, hands, ears and tongue are not trained to handle such responsibilities. But, since you have prayed for the highest achievements, some things will be taught to you. You will be sent to some workplace in order to get trained. It is just like playing cricket on the field. If someone hurls a spinning ball or a googly at you on the field, you say, "Why is this person hurling such a difficult ball at me even when he knows that I am a novice! He could have bowled an easier ball. Why is he spinning it so much?" The mind will complain in this manner. But after you attain the understanding, you will say, "This is actually the result of my prayers. I have got the opportunity to learn something new from this. Even though this kind of bowling has hurt me several times, I am beginning to understand the process of handling such a spinning ball (the problem). Earlier, I failed to understand even one out of ten such tough instances. But now I am able to grasp at least two to three times out of ten."

You may be getting hurt even now. But now at least you are getting the opportunity to understand the spin ball two to three times. This is the progress you have made. Therefore, now it can be hoped that a time will come when you will be able to recognize as well as play a difficult ball ten out of ten times. You will recognize the problem and will be able to solve it. Incidents are happening in your life so that you can reach such a state. When the mind says anything negative, you should be able to tell yourself, "Due to your prayers some problems are appearing in your life. Nature is also providing you the strength to solve them."

The mind has certain habits and tendencies due to which it is not able to hold the bat properly. But while playing, you need to break the habits of the mind. The remedy for this lies in giving a response filled with devotion and right behaviour. You need to observe all the balls of incidents coming towards you. Contemplate deeply on each of them so that you are able to decode the signal written on each of them. Do not hate the ball. The mind will feel that the ball is difficult; it can cause problems; it can break your bones. But you will say, "There is a message in these balls too. Let me first look for the message." In this way, by observing patience, you will learn from every incident because you would eventually understand that everything that happens is a result of your own prayers.

Impart understanding to the mind

We have received the mind and we have also received the resources to keep it under control. The string of love has been given to tie the monkeyish mind that should be fed with peanuts of understanding. As long as the monkey is eating the peanuts of understanding, it remains quiet.

After attaining true understanding, you may get troubled a bit by the incident. But you will not be troubled by the constant chattering and clamour of the mind as it used to happen earlier. Now, you will feel pain, but you will not feel pain over this pain. You will experience happiness, but you will never have the fear of losing it because now you know that the source of happiness lies within you.

Until you believe that the source of happiness lies outside you, you will feel uncertain about how long the happiness will last. You will have no guarantee whether you will experience the same feeling of happiness again. However, when you know that the source of happiness lies within you, you will not need any assurance for that. You can derive happiness whenever you want. But, necessary preparation is needed to arrive at such conviction. Incidents are happening in your life to strengthen this conviction. If you say that these incidents should happen next year instead of now, then you are postponing your progress by a year. After attaining understanding, you will say, "Whatever it is, let it happen today itself. Let it happen in this protected environment, where surrounding people are ready to help." In a protected environment, someone will help you stand up the moment you fall. In this way, take full advantage of the opportunities disguised in the garb of negative incidents.

While you are undergoing training, the mind will keep commenting on whatever it sees which will make you unhappy. At that time tell the mind, "Now you are complaining on whatever you see out of ignorance. But very soon you are only going to become the cause for happiness."

Organize the mind

As your mind is undergoing training, it would get stuck in its old viewpoints time and again. However, at such times you need to give it a new perspective. Remind it immediately of the understanding that has been imparted in this book. When you are in a happy mood, write down whatever you have understood. Keep some indications, reminders and self-suggestions ready for yourself. Note down in a diary what things you need to do when the mind gets stuck in something. Do not trust your mind when it is unhappy. Whatever the mind says at that time will be a lie only.

Keep a record of all the activities carried out by you from morning to night along with the time taken for each of them. This will help you to figure out how much free time is available with you. After getting this in writing, you will be surprised to see the amount of free time you are left with. Once you are clear about your schedule, ask yourself what all things you want to do in your life. Make a chart of them. Now see whether all those things fit in your available time. If you want to progress on all the facets of life, then determine in which areas change needs to be made, what work you wish to accomplish during this year.

Very often the mind wants to do everything at one time or nothing at all. You should not get stuck in either of these extremes. Plan your activities in such a way that they can be fitted into your timetable. For example, you want to sit in meditation for ten minutes. So, locate the free timeslot of ten minutes in your timetable and assign it for meditation. In this way, plan out all the pending activities in your timetable. By looking at the large volume of work, if the mind tries to escape by making excuses, make it agree to work in small bits and plan your work accordingly. Eventually, when you are able to complete your work on time, you will get the assurance from within that more work can be done now. Then gradually on your own you will increase your efficiency and capacity to work. In this way, you need to start getting work done from the mind using this new method.

After the mind gets ready for the highest and is trained to slim down, how will it look? Even if you think about this, you will like it so much that you will fall in love with such a mind. You will say, "Yes! This is how my mind should be."

What Next?

We have understood how the troublesome mind can be made the reason for great happiness in the longer run by getting it trained in the gym of the mind. In the next chapter, we will learn about how to train the inner mind.

22

Train the Inner Mind

When you meditate on your sense of beingness, you will reap the benefit of meditation. "What you focus on is what you become." This is the law of nature.

Those, who understand the importance of training the thoughts arising in the mind, are able to appreciate how crucial it is to train the mind for attaining Mission Earth. Those, who do not know the importance of this training, run away from this training.

Old programming of the inner mind

The mind is a victim of SICK programming. SICK is an abbreviation that represents **S**orrow borne out of **I**gnorance during **C**hildhood due to **K**razy beliefs inherited from parenting, neighbourhood and the surrounding environment. It is Krazy with a 'K' to indicate that these are beliefs that are baseless and have been formed due to an incorrect representation of incidents during childhood. Hence the mind expresses unhappiness upon hearing the old negative announcements.

Many a times, you may have noticed that all of a sudden you feel bored, dejected or sad. Many depressing thoughts occur to you such as, "What is the use of living? Why does this always happen with me? Why are people so bad?" Such thoughts emerge in you because of your inner mind's old programming. Due to lack of sensitivity at the subtler level, you do not even realize that your mind has announced, "Sorrow has arrived."

SICK programming in children takes place through parents, teachers, friends, advertisements, priests, politicians, etc. If a teacher repeatedly tells a child, "You are weak in mathematics" or "You always fall sick", then the child's inner mind believes what is being told. Always inspire children with positive thoughts because children are the future of this world.

Till today no one has formally trained you, no one has made you pray nor has anyone changed your thoughts. The actual reason for distress is the feeling of non-acceptance by your inner mind. The pre-determined framework of the mind does not accept certain things. It immediately announces: "This is good.", "That is bad." The mind visits the entire body and announces, "Sorrow has arrived" and you experience unhappiness due to this announcement. Now, through the medium of this book, you have been given the training on how to make the mind pure and unshakable.

New programming of the inner mind

In order to break the past programming and change your old thought patterns, it is very essential to give new thoughts to your mind. Today, the habit of contemplation and thinking power of people is reducing drastically. The old programming that has taken place since childhood has taken deep roots within you. To come out of this programming and break free of the established thinking structure, you need to give a new thought to yourself which is far more powerful. This can be done only by those who know the depth of the mind programming.

If you have trained your inner mind with a new thought or a new programming, your inner mind will declare, "The golden era of truth has arrived," instead of saying, "Sorrow has arrived." Even though the incident may seem to be negative from outside, the mind will make positive announcement (positive thoughts) internally.

Suppose that after being boxed on your face, you would begin to resemble your favourite actor or actress. What would be the announcement within your mind then? You would say, "Whatever happened was not bad. In fact, this is exactly what I need." Every incident is preparing you for your ultimate purpose. Hence, say to yourself, "Whatever happened was for my benefit."

Subtler aspects of programming the inner mind

What kind of feeling do you experience on your body when you are ill? You do not like anything at such times. The mind keeps on rejecting certain things. When you recover, you feel, "I recovered because I did not accept those things." This is the height of ignorance. There is no connection between you not accepting those things and your body recovering. In fact, the body naturally cures itself from illness. The old thinking pattern that if non-acceptance is shown then things get accomplished is wrong. The old thinking patterns remain the same even on growing up. But now, through the new training of the mind, you will know how to look at incidents and how to accomplish your Mission Earth.

You can change the programming of the inner mind by changing your thoughts and feelings. Those thoughts and feelings that are constantly repeated in the inner mind get manifested into reality. If you are afraid of a certain animal, you can remove the fear from your mind by giving repeated suggestions to your mind. In this manner, you can change your negative thoughts and feelings through the programming of your inner mind.

Numerous thoughts arise in your mind in a day. Your inner mind does not know which of these thoughts you would like to get into reality. In the confused state, it keeps creating appropriate and inappropriate conditions according to your changing thoughts. If you are able to clearly tell your inner mind what you really want, then it will quickly and easily create the appropriate condition for you. In order to give a clear indication to your inner mind, write what you want (a house, job, wealth, health, love, attention, designation, knowledge) in a diary. This will give a signal to your inner mind that no matter what you think throughout the day, you only want what you have written in your diary. This makes the job of the inner mind easier. Now write down in your diary the new programming you desire and the steps to achieve them. After this, repeat these thoughts every day in your mind for at least six months. After six months, check your diary to assess whether those thoughts, state, objects and success that you wanted have come true or not.

Utilise the services of your inner mind

If a bull (mind) is standing outside your door and you know that it has come to serve you, then you would say, "This bull is standing idle. It should be given some work. Let us make it draw oil from sesame seeds." However, if you do not know this, you will say, "Whose bull is this? Why has it come here? Drive it away. Why doesn't it run away?" If you clearly know that the bull has come for your service, then you would say, "Don't waste any time. Immediately engage it into some productive work." Then, towards the evening you will be very happy to see that it has extracted a lot of oil from the sesame seeds. Something worthwhile is done by it.

Every incident is preparing you according to the kind of training you need. You have understood from the example of being boxed that actually a punch was not for causing you pain. It was for shaping you. But when you were not aware of this, every punch used to cause you pain. Before the training of the inner mind, you were always in sorrow and complaining, "Why does this happen to me alone?" You were not able to utilise the services of the bull as mentioned in the above example. An untrained mind always sheds tears in every difficulty. But after training, tears of devotion begin to emerge from it.

The receptivity of the inner mind is enormous. It can grasp many things at the same time. It orchestrates physical activities, supports the intuitive mind, instructs the body according to the past training and also announces the arrival of joy or sorrow. After undergoing training, the same inner mind begins to work in a new and positive manner.

What Next?

In the next chapter, we will learn about how the mind can be brought under control and immersed in devotion.

23
Immerse the Mind in Devotion

Let us train the mind in such a manner that it walks the path of divine love, service, devotion, dedication and surrender, and helps us attain Mission Earth.

Several techniques and rituals have been invented to bring the mind under control. Some techniques have been proven to be effective. But rather than controlling the mind, the mind slipped into sluggishness using these techniques.

People have interpreted different meanings of mind control. They insist on controlling the mind through suppression. The same old techniques have been followed till date. The same old hymns have been chanted even today. Man neither wants to leave the old techniques nor does he become receptive for the new. The lovely bond that needs to be tied around the neck of the mind is not present. As a result, many rituals got formed. Attempts have been made to control the mind using these rituals. Success is achieved to some extent. But such a mind that has been forcibly brought under control cannot generate happiness. Due to this forceful control, it becomes dejected and depressed. In this way, the techniques for the mind control do not help in any way. Thus, the mind cannot be suppressed and put to work.

The mind which is brought under control through suppression

cannot become a cause of happiness. The mind works effectively when it is tied with something that can give it a joy. The mind needs to be tied with such a string by which it experiences joy and at the same time it does not dominate us. What string should be tied to the mind so that it can become the cause for supreme bliss and fulfilment? When the mind gets tied with the bond of unconditional love, it drinks the nectar of devotion. Thereafter, it becomes a servant and rows the boat of life without any dejection or depression and also experiences joy in the process.

If you want to understand the mind and all aspects related to it with the help of a symbol, then monkey can be a good example. The mind is like a monkey. You are the juggler who is making use of the mind. You are driving the mind.

Just like, you make use of microphone as a medium for making your voice heard over long distance. You are using the medium of the mind so as to express the voice of Self, the Consciousness, the Source. This is the highest possibility that can be attained by the mind. As you are making use of the mind, you are not the mind. The mind is a medium with the help of which you can cross over the illusory ocean of this material world.

Life is an opportunity and the mind is a boat. It is essential to get across this illusory ocean of the material world in this very lifetime with the help of the mind. What is the point in reaching there after death? Attain the highest possibility of human life, the state of liberation, while you are still alive on this Earth. The mind needs to be tied with the loving bond of divine devotion for this.

When the mind is focused on the external world, it is a hypocritical devotee. But, when the mind turns within, it transforms into a true devotee. As the mind immerses deeper into the nectar of divine devotion, it gradually transforms into a devotee of the highest order.

Devotion brings about complete transformation

As the feeling of devotion awakens in the mind, man begins to get liberated from this illusory world. Unconditional love and unconditional reverence are characteristics of divine devotion. Devotion transforms man into love itself. The mind becomes pure and virtuous by walking on the path of devotion. The joy derived by giving a response filled with devotion is true bliss in itself. Even though there is nothing for the ego in giving devotional response, the mind feels immense joy. In devotion, the mind begins to dissolve and breaks free from the shackles of the worldly desires, lust and pleasures. It then attains the feeling of love and the joy of freedom.

No sooner the mind is filled with divine devotion than your entire life is filled with the feeling of gratitude and the ego of the mind begins to dissolve. The feeling of 'I' in the mind dies and the veil of ignorance is lifted. The mind is a curtain between the devotee and God. It surrenders by singing hymns in praise of God. Thereby it becomes one with God. This state is known as Self-realization. Keep this goal in mind and begin to practice divine devotion.

When the mind never gets tired of praising the Self, the Consciousness, only then it can be said that the mind is in love with God, the mind has attained divine devotion. In true devotion, one needs to think at every moment as to whom he is responding to and whose work is being done. Thus, devotion breaks the unconscious state of the mind. In divine devotion alone man is able to think, "How can I fulfil what God wants out of me?"

Divine devotion is a gift given to man. This gift serves as a constant reminder of the Self until the state of Self-realization is attained by him. In devotion, the mind is transformed into a state of bright ignorance and brought into the original primal state. The mind and in turn the ego then surrenders happily in true devotion.

You have bowed down your head at holy places. But have you ever bowed down your mind? Have you ever surrendered your thoughts? Have you ever attained thoughtless state at that time? Mind is the sole obstacle in attaining the truth. You wish to get rid of the mind. Holy places serve as means to achieve this purpose and attain the supreme truth. Unfortunately, they are losing their original intention and significance today.

Devotion is a seed as well as a fruit in itself. It is complete in itself. Mind gets immersed in devotion and body is used as a medium for that. Majority of people commonly believe that God is pleased with them when they engage in devotion. But the converse is true. In reality, when God is pleased with you, devotion awakens within you. If devotion is overflowing through you, then have faith that God is indeed pleased with you. Along with devotion, if man keeps constantly praying to God to free him from the delusion of this illusory world, then very soon he will get free from all the dramas of the mind.

When the mind attains devotion and understanding, the devotion does not stop at blind devotion but turns into unconditional devotion. Love transcends lust and conditional love. Prayer does not become a begging but turns into gratitude. Compassion does not remain a pity, but transforms into unconditional forgiveness. Trust does not remain blind faith, but transforms into unconditional faith. Rather than expression of feelings as tears of sorrow, feelings turn into unconditional happiness. Desires no longer become a pain for the mind, but turn into happy thoughts. Friendship changes from being a bondage to being a congregation of truth seekers. Death does not become an end of life, but a milestone for bright life and a timeless state of being which is also called as *samadhi*. Thoughts no longer somersault. Instead, they serve as a mirror for Self to know Himself. Memory no longer reminds of the past to cause a feeling of guilt. It becomes a rosary for remembering God (Self Remembrance).

When the mind gets deeply immersed in the ocean of devotion, all things of the world seem insignificant to it. Material gifts, status, fame, power or any other worldly pleasures do not attract it anymore. Instead, it finds everlasting bliss in divine devotion and lives life by completely being absorbed in it. Those, who have received the gift of divine devotion in their life, are very lucky because they get completely free from the somersaulting thoughts, vices and bad tendencies of the mind and become one with God. Just as water sprinkled on the petals of a lotus flower subsides immediately, through a little devotion, no disorder remains in the mind.

Search for unconditional love

You need to have divine devotion towards that thing which constantly loves you at each and every moment. No matter whether you perform good or bad deeds, that thing still loves you. Do you know that this inner friend likes you a lot? This friend is not the type who will slow down your breath or stop it if you perform bad deeds or would speed up your breath if you perform good deeds. Who is that within you which loves you incessantly? You need to have devotion for that thing.

Let us understand this with an example of a priest. Whenever the priest used to perform prayers at home, his neighbour used to yell and shout during that precise period in order to trouble him. One day the priest was seething with anger and rushed to the neighbour's house to beat him up. Before he could enter the neighbour's house, a voice came from within, "Do not touch my friend." As soon as he heard this voice, he turned back home. The neighbour was very surprised to see that.

The neighbour then stopped the priest in between and asked, "You came in seething with anger. But you are returning without venting your anger. What is the reason?" The priest smiled and said, "Many thanks to you! Because of you, this is the first time that I could hear God's voice." The neighbour asked in amazement, "God's voice!? What did God say?" The priest honestly told him, "God said, "Do not touch my friend". Hence, I was obeying God's order and was quietly returning home. This union with God has happened because of you. Hence, thank you very much."

The next day the neighbour came to the priest and bowed down to him. He said, "I am leaving." Now it was the priest's turn to get surprised. He asked, "Where are you going?" With his voice choked with emotion, the neighbour replied, "I am leaving in search of that very friend who protects me and loves me so much."

What is that thing within us which constantly loves us unconditionally no matter what? Loving that very love is divine devotion. If the mind gets immersed in such devotion, it will no longer trouble us. There is that thing within all of us which constantly loves us while we are idle or in action. Everyone wishes to receive the power of that loving entity which constantly loves us. We have to learn to love this very supreme power, the Source, the Consciousness.

In fact, you seek this unconditional love in all your relations too. When the mind surrenders in love, becomes quiet and remains in the supreme state of silence, then Self becomes aware of Self. This is not the experience which is experienced through the senses. It is the experience, the rhythm of music, which is constantly running within you. But people believe themselves to be the mind. Hence, they want to please the mind. They just know - "If the mind is happy, then I am happy." They trust only in the power of the mind. They use intellect and strength to resolve the problems of their life. But those who have tasted divine devotion in their lives know that the power of devotion is the greatest power and true love awakens with divine devotion only. Until devotion awakens within you, you do not appreciate devotion. But once it awakens, then nothing in the world appears to be better than it.

Master your mind through divine devotion

To master the mind is equivalent to controlling the mind. This control needs to be exercised not through force and power, but through patience and understanding. Otherwise, some people try to forcefully control their mind. As a result, rather than getting the mind under control, it goes out of control. For example, one goes to a temple and thinks, "Bad thoughts should not arise in my mind while I am in the temple. I am such an ardent devotee of God, so I should always have pure thoughts, etc." At that moment, the more one tries to stop such thoughts, the more such thoughts crop up in his mind. Success is achieved not by rebuking or demeaning the mind, but by awakening divine devotion in it.

Give your mind truth thoughts

You need to train your mind in such a way that it will do its self-enquiry on its own without any external trigger and will dissolve itself. Once the mind starts liking the act of getting dissolved, then Self experiences Self. What is needed is a new habit of meditation.

Thoughts arise consistently in the mind. The arising of thoughts is not bad. After all, the mind is there to have thoughts only. It is a means to bring about thoughts. Thus, the tool in the form of the mind is functioning perfectly. We just need to provide some direction to it. In order to provide direction to the mind, one more appropriate thought needs to be produced. It is not advised to stop thinking. On the contrary, since you are already thinking, it is advised to have new truth thoughts.

When a child breaks things, you tell him not to do so. But still he continues with his mischief. Then the child is asked to break some more things as well. The child feels awkward with this and immediately calms down. In the same way, as you are already thinking, have some more thoughts related to truth. Think, "Who is thinking all these thoughts?" The mind which is engaged in having all other thoughts should be trained to have truth thoughts. This will give a new, right direction to the mind.

What Next?

In the next chapter, we will learn about how to sublimate the mind through Self-expression.

24

Sublimate the Mind Through Self-Expression

Just as water sprinkled on the petals of a lotus flower subsides immediately, through a little devotion no disorder remains in the mind.

The path of winning over the mind by making it win is straightforward and simple. Let us understand this with the help of a story. There was a village of monkey charmers. They earned their living by making their pet monkeys perform tricks to entertain people. They used to visit neighbouring villages every day to perform shows. After earning some money, they would return home in the evening. The monkeys were trained to perform tricks and were tied with ropes. However, they could snap the rope at will and indulge in their whims and fancies. The monkeys were trained so as to not snap the rope while performing. A monkey charmer would feed his monkey after returning home in the evening. When the monkey was idle, it would free itself from the rope and engage in mischief. It used to poke around things in the house and leave them strewn all around. The monkey charmer would be upset with this. He would repeatedly tie the monkey with the rope and the monkey would again open the rope whenever it wanted. The monkey had got habituated to playing such pranks.

One fine day, the monkey charmer met a guide. He narrated all his woes and troubles to him and asked for a remedy. The guide told him, "There is a solution. But you need to first become ready to receive it. Your eligibility is extremely important." The monkey charmer showed his readiness. He proved his eligibility. The guide then told him, "If you follow the road that cuts through the mountains and forests, you will reach a temple. There is a large pillar in the temple. Atop this pillar is a diamond. The touch of that diamond alone can change this mischievous habit of the monkey forever."

The monkey charmer asked the guide, "If there are many pillars in the temple, how will I recognize the right one?" The guide replied, "The pillar that holds the diamond can be distinguished by several caterpillars climbing on it. The caterpillars that reach the top of the pillar will turn into butterflies. They keep falling off to the ground and then resume their ascent again. In this manner, they continue their journey in an effort to reach the diamond. The caterpillars that fail to access the diamond perish before they turn into butterflies. They are never able to take flight. You need to get the monkey to climb this pillar and throw the diamond at you. That diamond alone can solve all your problems. It will change monkey's habit of mischief. The monkey will then surrender in divine devotion."

The monkey charmer was elated upon hearing about this solution. He began his journey with the monkey through the forest towards the temple. After all, if a small caterpillar could climb that pillar, albeit taking several years to do so, his monkey would climb it in a minute! But during the journey, the monkey escaped the rope and wandered into the jungle. It began to play around with the scorpions and snakes in the dense jungle. Sometimes it ate leaves of marijuana. At times, it drank the intoxicating water from the streams, thereby corrupting its intellect. Now, the monkey was in a state of disarray.

The monkey charmer somehow managed to make the monkey climb the pillar. Though the monkey could reach the top, it failed to recognize the diamond. The diamond appeared to be a piece of charcoal to it because it did not have the discerning eye to recognize the diamond. The monkey had to be trained in order to recognize the diamond. The guide could guide and train the monkey because he had recognition of the diamond. As a result of this training, the monkey did not break free off the rope. It stopped wandering into the jungle. It stayed away from eating the leaves of marijuana. It did not drink the intoxicating water from the streams of the jungle.

Being safeguarded from all the risks and with proper training, the monkey could reach the diamond atop the pillar. When this diamond was attached to the rope tied around the monkey's neck, the monkey happily stayed bonded by the rope. All its crazy activities came to an end. Thereafter, the monkey charmer led a happy and content life and so did his monkey.

The story of the monkey charmer is not someone else's story; it is your very own. You are the monkey charmer, and the monkey is the mind. As long as you are busy doing your work, your intuitive mind is at work. For example, when a housewife, who is busy with her household chores, becomes free from work, she may begin to complain, "Why is my life so? Do I have to work this way all my life? Am I a servant?" In this way, the mind frees itself from the rope and plays mischief, thereby causing unhappiness. Whenever it finds time, it keeps entangling itself.

The mind is like a monkey within you. If it were outside, you could have confronted it. But since it is within, a guide is needed to train it. Because of the mind, crazy ego awakens in man. Thoughts of hatred, ill-will and fear trouble him. Ignorance deludes him. Lethargy troubles him. As a result, man's intellect malfunctions. The mind should not be allowed to come in contact with these things. It should be trained to keep away from bad company and illusory attractions. With this, the intellect will get safeguarded.

As the intellect gets safeguarded and you recognize the opportunity that life is offering you, it becomes very easy for you to attain Mission Earth. The mind then becomes steadfast, obedient, untainted and loving. It gets bonded with the rope of love, divine devotion for the Self. It surrenders itself in love of the Self. The truth, the Consciousness which was veiled by the ignorance of the mind shines forth. Thereafter, the mind becomes instrumental in expressing the qualities of the Self. This is the path of winning over the mind by making the mind win. This is the ultimate method of eliminating the mind.

What Next?

In the next chapter, we will learn about the world of the mind and the world when the mind surrenders.

25

If You Have Faith, You Will See

When the mind is tied with the bond of bright unconditional love,
then it will drink the nectar of divine devotion, and enthusiastically
it will serve to ply the oars of the boat of life.
Also, it will experience bliss in the process.

Every world has its own rules. The mind's world is the world of Science. The mind examines everything in the laboratory. All things of the world are on table in the mind's laboratory. The mind is their examiner. It enquires, "What is this thing. How does it work?" This is the world of the mind. The mind is a scientist, and the rule of Science is: First see and then believe. This is why the mind is not able to believe in the truth without seeing it.

This is not the case in the world of no-mind. The rule here is: If you have faith, you will see. In this world, the mind itself is on the laboratory table.

When the mind is the scientist who investigates, the rules are different. But, when the mind (scientist) itself is on the laboratory table and experiments are being conducted on it, the rules are different. But even when the mind lies on the laboratory table, it wishes that its rules work here too. Before becoming unconscious, it wants to give some instructions, "This should happen… That should happen... Do this... Don't do this..., etc." The poor mind is on the surgery table. The rule of its world, "First see and then believe" is of no use then.

The rule of the no-mind world is: "If you believe, you shall see." Faith is therefore very important. When the mind is told of an incident that happened when it was not there, it does not believe it. According to the rules of the no-mind world, the mind needs to first believe. When faith increases, then the sense of beingness is clearly experienced. If someone were to tell you in the beginning itself that this is how the sense of being (experience of Self) is, the mind will not believe it. As the mind develops strong faith, it will begin to understand the depth of surrendering.

Let us understand this further. Whenever you experience something, the mind that says, "I am experiencing this" is absent. But after the experience has taken place, the mind comes in and says, "I experienced this." It tries to label the experience as good or bad. Imagine that you have gone to an amusement park. You are taking a joy ride in a giant wheel. While the ride is going on, you experience something. At that moment your mind does not come in and say, "This experience is happening with me." This is because the mind is not there at that moment. There are no thoughts at that moment which comment on the experience. But later, the mind, which has not experienced anything, comes in and says, "Today I had such and such experience." In this manner, the mind retrieves the memory of the experience from the memory bank and associates itself with it. Everyone has been given the power of memory. Every incident that takes place with you gets stored in your memory. The mind remembers the incident from this memory and claims that experience to be its own. It says, "I had this experience." If the mind is told that it was not there at that time, it does not believe it.

You happen to sit in meditation. Once the meditation is over, your mind comes and says, "I had such an experience. I will again sit in meditation tomorrow and will have the same experience." However, the fact is that when you had that experience, your mind was not there. At that time, the mind did not even know that such an experience was going to occur. But later on it feels, "I had become thoughtless. I felt such and such experience. I will again sit tomorrow and bring back the same experience." The next day the mind continues with meditation and waits for the same experience. It says, "Nothing has happened till now. Nothing is happening today."

The mind fails to realize that it was due to its absence that the experience of Self was witnessed. The mind becomes an obstacle in the attainment of the experience of Self. The mind must attain the understanding that the experience of Self can happen only when it is absent. If the mind has faith in this understanding, it will agree to get into the state of stillness which is beyond noise and silence.

Faith is extremely important in the process of attaining the experience of Self because the mind lives in the illusion that it experienced Self. The mind refuses to understand that it was absent when the experience happened. Until it has strong faith, it will keep saying, "How can this be? I had the experience of Self. I myself felt it." However, the mind has no experience of Self in reality. Right now, the experience of Self can be attained, but the biggest obstacle in experiencing it, is the mind. The mind does not need to turn back and see whether the experience is there or not. But the mind keeps thinking, "How is the experience of Self? Let me also see." In this manner, the mind itself becomes an obstacle. If the mind stops checking and surrenders completely, then Self-realization is possible. Imagine that there is an idol behind you, and the person in front of you wants to see it. You need to bow down then alone the person can see the idol. When the mind gets fully convinced about this and has strong faith on the Guru who guides him, it will then say, "Now I will not turn back and see. I will not check the experience. I will dissolve in silence. I will no more be present." In this manner, when the mind surrenders, Self experiences Self.

The thinner of knowledge

The contrast mind engages in a lot of deceit. It becomes the master when actually it is the servant. It tries to see God within us. It says, "Where is God? Where is the truth? I too want to see God." This is just like the eye wants to see the eye itself, but cannot see it. Similarly, the contrast mind wants to see God (Self, experience of beingness, the Consciousness, the Source). The contrast mind needs to be given the understanding that God is already present within us, but the contrast mind itself has become an obstacle in between. If the contrast mind surrenders, Self will become aware of Self.

When the contrast mind moves aside, the experience of beingness is there. Even then the contrast mind comes in between, and makes you experience something else. It tries to entangle you in it. The contrast mind tries all the crooked tricks from its side. Assume that the contrast mind has fifty tricks. While meditating if you begin to feel some experience like seeing some light, understand that the contrast mind has shown you one of its tricks. If you do not get trapped in its tricks, you will be happy. Then you will wish that the contrast mind quickly plays out all of its fifty tricks so that you become the master of your mind.

The contrast mind has to be quickly got rid of so that Self experiences Self. The mind plays the role of glue between Self and the body. Self has got badly stuck to the body due to the contrast mind. It is now thinking itself to be the body and is living in the body alone. The day Self detaches itself from the body, Self will become aware of Self. It is therefore important for the glue between Self and the body to melt. The mind has to drop. A thinner of knowledge is required for this purpose. Once the glue (mind) melts, Self will be liberated from the body, and you will be established in the experience of Self forever and will attain the supreme bliss.

What Next?

In the next chapter, we will learn about how the mind is not a seer but a sight.

26

The Mind is Not the Seer, But the Sight

If mystical powers can be attained through the power of the mind, then the supreme truth can also be attained through it. If the attunement of the mind for materialism can give us everything in this illusory world, then the Creator of this world can also be attained through bright devotion.

In order to conquer over the mind, you need to remove the word 'I', the false 'I' from the mind which keeps arising time and again in the mind. Learn how to eliminate this false 'I'. Reduce the use of the word 'I' from your conversations as much as you can. Whenever you get thoughts such as, "I am feeling sad", "I am getting bored", "I am feeling depressed", remove the word 'I' from these thoughts. When thoughts of boredom, sorrow, stress, depression, etc. arise, you get attached to them. This attachment alone is the cause of sorrow. As soon as thoughts of sorrow, depression and anxiety arise within you, you should immediately tell yourself, "Thoughts of sorrow are passing through me. Thoughts of depression and anxiety are passing by."

Once in a day, ask yourself, "What thoughts are passing through me at this moment?" You will then observe that as you begin this exercise, you will no longer feel the same amount of distress as you used to feel earlier due to these troubling thoughts. In a short span of time, you will find various kinds of thoughts passing through your mind. You will become aware about the current state of your mind and the number of times the states keep changing. The question will then arise within you, "Should this mind be trusted?" The answer will be "No". The mind which has been observed to change into so many different forms throughout the day just cannot be trusted.

Induce the understanding of 'I' into the mind

You need to ingrain the understanding of the true 'I' into your mind. Who is the real 'I' within you? If you ask someone, "Who are you?" she would promptly tell her name as, "I am Ms. Monica." Now if you explain her that she is not Ms. Monica in reality. She has first come in this world, and the name was given to her later. She will not agree to it. If you ask a military officer, "Who are you?" he may reply, "I am Brigadier Samir." If you tell him, "You are not a brigadier. This is only a designation given to you," he will not be ready to believe you. Many labels such as Brigadier, Colonel, Doctor get assigned due to which one forgets his true nature.

Am I this body that I am carrying around everywhere? Perform a small experiment to understand this. Keep aside this book for a minute and carry out this experiment. But before you proceed, first understand the experiment:

Stretch out your hand. Look at it and ask yourself, "Am I this hand?" Keep asking this question to your mind repeatedly and listen to the answer that comes to you. The answer will be, "No, I am not this hand." When you have seen your entire hand, see your arms, feet, legs… see all parts of your body and keep asking yourself, "Am I this…?"

You will get a jolt and will be left wondering, "If I am not all this, then who am I?" Knowing this by intellect is of no consequence.

Unless you know it through your experience, the answer is not complete. This experience of Self is not on the body. Many people try to seek this experience on the body. When they perform some breathing exercises, they feel relieved from stress. They feel their body has become light. They feel good about that experience. But, it is the experience of sensations on the body. Many people are misled due to such experiences. They mistake the pleasant experience on the body to be the experience of Self. But what is being discussed here is not the experience of the body, but the experience that is beyond the body-mind-intellect. This experience does not happen on the body, but is experienced because of the body. By observing each part of your body in this manner, this experiment will be successful. This experiment will give you a new insight. In this manner, your attachment to the body will diminish, and you will begin to know your true Self. After knowing who you truly are, you will become the master of your mind, not its slave.

The mind is not the seer, but the sight

If someone says, "I have seen God," then understand that it was an object that he was talking about. This is because whatever the mind sees becomes an object. You see all the objects of this world through your eyes including your body. This implies that your body too is an object. You need to know the one who is seeing these objects. To reveal this secret, the contrast mind has to drop, and you need to go beyond the mind. The mind wants to play the role of a seer. It wants to witness and see the truth. But this desire of the mind is never fulfilled. The truth has always been present within you, but it will know itself only when the mind surrenders and dissolves itself.

After knowing the truth, the false 'I' drops. For this to happen, the mind needs to become silent. However, if the mind is asked to become silent, it would become even more troubled. As the mind is already restless, it will grow even more restless thinking that it now needs to become silent too. Hence, it is only asked to listen to the truth discourses, contemplate on the truth and read about it. On knowing the truth, happiness and the state of stillness which is beyond noise and silence automatically enhances, and the mind begins to drop.

When you are in deep meditation, often referred to as samadhi, the feeling of beingness ('I am' ness) is experienced. In that state, the body, mind and thoughts are not present. The sensation of the body and the mind vanishes and the experience of bright universal 'I' is experienced. When such a state is attained, the mind is not present and hence the experience is predominant. At that moment, it is experienced that I am even without the body or the mind; that my beingness does not depend on the mind or the body. Strong faith is needed to have this conviction. Through the practice of meditation and samadhi, one needs to experience that the real 'I' exists even without the body and the mind.

After coming out from samadhi, the mind returns and declares, "What an experience! How blissful I felt!" The mind says this by remembering the experience from the memory. It feels happy to recall the experience. Actually, the mind has not seen the experience, still it becomes extremely happy. Even though the mind has not seen the treasure, it feels so happy. When does this happen? This happens when the mind becomes ready to surrender.

Seek happiness from the origin

Everyone in this world is in search of true happiness. Every human being is blessed with a great gift that helps him seek this happiness. He needs to just see this gift and derive happiness. You can derive as much joy as you want from this gift. Now, it is up to you, how much joy you want to derive. This gift is such that the more you look at it, the more your happiness increases. This is an internal gift. External gifts are not of such nature. If someone gifts you something, you do not see it again and again. If the mind goes within, then you can experience this bliss again and again. It is not that when the mind turns within, the external activities in the outside world will come to a standstill. In fact, when the mind is turned within, external activities will happen in a better and smoother way without stress and with ease using the intuitive mind.

This internal boon is also referred to as the 'Origin'. Origin means the source of each and every thing, i.e. Self, truth, the Consciousness. It is also called as 'Imperishable', that which cannot perish. The body can perish, but the Origin can never perish. The day man experiences the Origin, his fear of death will vanish that very moment. In the Origin, there are no thoughts of duality. It has the language of One or Oneness only. The language of duality is that of the contrast mind. It says, "good", if you understand some particular thing, and "bad" if you do not understand it. The mind is the ribbon with which the gift has been tied and is not opening up.

When does the mind surrender?

You need to first make the mind understand, "Please help by not doing anything." The problem starts when the mind tries to help. What help does the mind offer? When an incident occurs, it says, "I did it." As long as the mind holds onto the ignorance that it is doing everything, it feels stressed about the future. The mind thinks, "If I have done everything till now, then I will have to do everything in the future too." The day it understands that it has not done anything till date, all the burden of future responsibilities will vanish. For example, a woman who is taking care of her child thinks that she has taken care of the child till now and will need to do the same in the future too. She is told, "You were not the one who took care of the child. Self was taking care of it since the beginning." This implies that she need not have to do it in the future too. Similarly, the contrast mind should be given the understanding that till today it has not done anything and later on also it has to do nothing. That's it! It just needs to remain silent. On attaining this understanding, the mind will become silent. It will surrender before the Origin because the Origin alone is the doer of all actions.

What Next?

In the next chapter, we will learn about how to silence the mind.

27

Silence the Mind

The rule of the no-mind world is: If you believe, you shall see.

Someone had guests at their house. Their two children were busy doing some work inside the house. They called out the children to meet up with the guests. The elder son was given full opportunity to demonstrate his skills in front of the guests. It was natural for the elder son to know something more than the younger one. Hence, more opportunity was given to him. Their parents thought that the younger son was not skilled enough, so less attention was given to him. The elder son enthusiastically showed his paper craft to the guests. The younger one also tried to show his paper craft, but he was asked to keep quiet. Then, the elder son showed his paintings. The younger one also tried to show. However, he was hushed up. No one heard him. In this way, the elder son exhibited all his talents in front of the guests and the younger one did not get any chance to exhibit his talents. He was asked to keep quiet. Nobody paid attention to him. He jumped around restlessly and wanted to say something.

The experience of beingness, the aliveness within us is like the younger son. It wants to tell us something. It keeps calling out to us, "Please pay attention to me…" But we do not feel that anything significant will happen by paying attention to it, or that the guests (people of the world) will be impressed. Even if we give it a chance, we do not believe that it will do something good. We think, "It will surely mess up things. Who knows what untoward things it might say in the talent show and the guests could become upset." You know that children say anything in front of the guests.

Naughty children keep messing up something or the other. Therefore, their parents either instruct them in advance or they do not let the children speak in front of the guests. They are unsure about how the children will respond in front of the guests. They do not want to get into any embarrassing situation due to their children's misbehaviour. They do not want the guests to comment on the upbringing of their children, lack of discipline in their children. The younger son wants attention from the guests. However, the elder son gets more attention.

Here, the elder son represents the mind which is interested in showing off its arts and talents. Initially, people value it more believing it to be of great use. After all, they have become successful and have earned worldly achievements with the help of the mind. Then someone tells them, "This is not the reality. There is something else other than this. When you are associated with it, you can experience happiness and contentment. That happiness will be different from all other joys. Such happiness is experienced only when you do what you have come to do on Earth." Only then you begin your journey beyond the mind and pay attention to the younger son (experience of beingness, Self, the Consciousness, the Source).

The scene described in the above example explains the internal state of the two sons. The elder son symbolizes the mind that is being shown to the guests. It has attracted everyone's attention. What is the art work of the mind? What are the pictures painted by the mind? What is the clay work of the mind? What is the talent show of the mind? You see that every day. Entertainment of the mind is liked by all.

The world around you is the world of the mind. When you see the sensual attractions of this world, you easily and quickly get entangled in them. While passing by a road, you get engrossed in whatever you see. That's the present state of the mind! Negative thoughts begin instantly. You just do not realize how much time is wasted in this. When awakening dawns in you, you begin to realize how you got completely lost in those scenes. Now, you need to learn where to focus your attention after shifting it from your thoughts. Those who contemplate, easily realize how to do it. By contemplation, one can immediately shift the focus from the mind's chattering.

When the elder son (mind) is showing his art work, your attention is focused on that alone because you have been trained to focus there. You get deluded by whatever you see, speak and hear from morning to evening. When the mind gets trained to remain silent for a while, Self experiences Self. This experience has been given different names such as God, Self-witness, Self, truth, the Consciousness, the Source.

Focus your attention on the younger son

Despite having so many distractions in the world, why would you want to focus your attention on the younger son (Self) and go within? The thought of going within will not even occur to you. Man gets so lured by the objects of entertainment that his attention always remains outside. He prays only to attain objects of pleasure and comfort. Man makes such prayers due to lack of understanding. As you understand that the joy you derive by focussing on Self is far greater and permanent in nature than the temporary happiness you derive by focussing on the mind, you shift your focus to Self. You start developing faith in it. You realize that the whole game of the world is meant to attain the experience of truth and one is ought to focus the attention there alone. Now, your prayers will be to attain that experience alone. With this understanding and constant focus on Self, the mind begins to surrender. It becomes silent.

With constant focus on Self, you enter into a doorway passing through which a new world reveals before you. The mind will not wish to enter this doorway. It will make excuses. It will try to misguide you. It will try to convince you that you will benefit a lot by obeying it. However logical and correct its arguments might sound, you ought not to listen to it at this juncture. Only divine devotion can save you from this constant acrobatics of the mind. Knowledge alone cannot protect you from this churning of the mind. Hence, it is essential to have devotion along with knowledge in order to silence the mind.

What Next?

In the next chapter, we will learn some questions and answers about the mind.

28
Questions and Answers

Let us go through some questions on the mind and their profound answers which will give you some more understanding and insights for training and transcending your mind.

Q. 1: Can the mind know God?

A: Self is beyond the mind. The mind can never know Self. When the mind remains silent, then Self becomes aware of Self. But the mind never accepts the fact that it is unaware about something which already exists. It is similar to the fact that sometimes people feel ashamed to say that they do not know something. If we do not know something, then we should be able to clearly say, "I don't know it." But they give weird answers to avoid embarrassment.

For example, a person was not able to attain success despite working very hard for it. He met some people in order to find the reason for the same. One person told him, "Your fate is not in your favour. Hence, you are not able to attain success." Some other person told him, "You must have committed certain bad deeds in your past lifetime. Hence, success is eluding you in this lifetime." Thus, instead of saying, "I don't know", answers backed by beliefs were given related to luck, destiny or past lifetimes. Why should one be embarrassed to say, "I don't know"? Instead of accepting the fact that they do not know, people give wrong answers.

For instance, a child asks a question to his father. If the father does not know the answer, he should say, "I too do not know the answer to this question. So come on son, let us look for the answer together." A person asked his friend, "Why do dewdrops appear on the surface of leaves and plants in the morning?" His friend replied, "The Earth perspires a lot as it has to rotate for the whole day. The sweat in turn appears in the form of dewdrops on the leaves." Here too, instead of saying, "I don't know", some ridiculous answer is given.

In this way, people give readymade legacy answers related to destiny, heaven, the result of deeds from past lifetimes, etc. If this birth is the result of deeds performed in the past lives, then what was the cause of the first birth? Due to which deeds would the first birth have taken place? If this question is asked to someone, then he is afraid to admit that he does not know the answer and continues to dish out speculative answers. In fact, such answers have only led to various imaginations about God. The mind can imagine about God, but cannot experience God. The eye glasses cannot see the eyes. The mind is the eye glasses of God. Hence, the mind can never see God. When the mind surrenders and becomes silent (no-mind) through contemplation and understanding, then Self becomes aware of Self. God experiences Himself.

Q. 2: Am I distinct from the mind?

A: Yes, you and the mind are distinct entities. You see your mind making excuses. You see the mind becoming sad and unhappy. When you say, "I am being humiliated, my mind is sad," who is it that is saying this? It cannot be the mind! Like, if someone says, "My pen is not working," then 'I' cannot be the pen. I am seeing the pen go dry. It means – I am the seer. Similarly, you are seeing the mind at work, being in doubt, getting upset and becoming sad. This implies that you are not the mind. Then who is it that is watching the mind? Try to get hold of it, right now, this very moment.

Q. 3: My mind does not go within. Or sometimes it does and sometimes it does not.

A: The mind does not go within because it is unaware of what lies within. The outside world is well known to all. Everyone goes to places like home, workplace, shops, temples, etc. You tend to go to those places which you know and tend to avoid the places that are unknown to you. Hence, make the unknown known. Know what lies within. The more you listen to the truth, read and contemplate on the truth, the more you will understand what is within and you will begin to speak to your inner seat of beingness which can be felt in the area around the heart. You will find inspiration to go within. You will feel eager to enter into the state of stillness. Through this practice, you will be so enthusiastic to go into the state of stillness that you will feel, "When do I go into silence? When will I get the time? When will I go within?" Until this state arrives, tell your mind, "The world inside is unknown, which is why the mind does not feel like going inside. But, this is possible through practice. I shall sit for meditation every day."

Your mind sometimes goes within and sometimes it does not. It is good that it goes within at least sometimes. There are many in whom the mind simply does not go within. Very soon, this 'sometimes' will become 'just now'. If somebody asks you, "Did you go within?" You will reply, "I am just returning from there." If you are asked, "Did you go to the temple?" you would reply, "That is where I am coming from!" When you wake up from sleep and are asked, "Have you been to the temple?" your reply would still be, "I am just coming from there." This implies that the mind is repeatedly going within.

Q. 4: When Self-realization happens, the contrast mind dies. What exactly happens to the contrast mind?

A: The contrast mind is the mind that is constantly engaged in comparing. What happens when this mind dies? Understand this with the help of a story of a rabbit. A rabbit fought with a lion in a jungle.

The lion had warned all the animals of the jungle, "If you do not want me to kill all the animals in the forest, send one animal a day as a meal to my cave." Thus, every day an animal would go to the lion and become the lion's meal. When it was the rabbit's turn, it cleverly took the lion to a well and smartly managed to make the lion jump and drown in the well.

The lion symbolizes the contrast mind that has been introduced in man. What happened in the jungle when the contrast mind (lion) died? All the animals that lived in fear became fearless. When the contrast mind dies, you become fearless. After the lion's death, all the animals of the forest began to live in harmony with love. Similarly, with the death of the contrast mind, you get free of conditional love and hatred and begin to live in bright love and harmony with the entire world.

The contrast mind (lion) thinks that this rabbit is a tiny creature, what can it do?! When bigger animals like elephants could do nothing, what can this rabbit do?! The contrast mind indulges in comparisons and draws conclusions. By listening to others, it lets loose the reins of its imagination. After listening to someone, it says, "What kind of an answer is this? This answer is not right." In this manner, it remains entangled in the mesh of its own assumptions and imaginations.

Without getting into the details of how did the lion fall into the well, understand one thing. When the contrast mind dies, comparisons stop. Fearlessness comes in. You begin giving and receiving happiness. You become instrumental for others to attain the truth. This is known as the death of the contrast mind, where thoughts of comparison, judgment and duality stop.

Q. 5: Do thoughts stop after the contrast mind dies?

A: Thoughts do not stop after the contrast mind dies. Thoughts do occur. But those thoughts that used to arise out of the belief that you are the body, stop arising. If your mind is fed with the thought that a doughnut is ring-shaped, then whenever you think of a doughnut, you will only think of it in a ring shape.

Thoughts that stem from such beliefs will stop after the death of the contrast mind. As long as you lead your life thinking yourself to be the body, thoughts like, "Where should I go? What should I do? What will become of me in the future?" arise This is because you believe yourself to be the body. When you consider yourself to be the body, the thoughts you get are: "My body should get everything. If I do not get everything, then my life is futile." This is how everyone speaks with reference to the body and says, "My colour is so and so… my height is so and so… my voice is so and so… I am like this…" Before the death of the contrast mind, you always thought by assuming yourself to be the body and were vacillating in your assumptions and imaginations. You had a fixed idea about doughnut being ring-shaped, so thoughts used to occur in the same manner. Even in your dreams, if you thought of a doughnut, you saw it in the same shape and size. After the contrast mind dies, such thoughts will stop coming. New, fresh thoughts will begin to occur. They will be thoughts filled with happiness. Going forward, thoughts will not occur to you; you will bring them in.

Q. 6: Does the falling silent of the mind imply that one has got back to his true nature, Self? Because whenever I try to return to Self, the mind starts chattering or singing hymns. So what must be done? Even if the thoughtless state is attained, it is only for a few moments.

A: It is true that the mind falling silent means being in the experience of Self. The mind going within symbolizes the mind falling silent or in the state of stillness which is beyond noise and silence. There is a saying: "If your mind is within, then you are *Mahavira*." ('*Mahavira*' here implies the one who possesses supreme courage and has thereby mastered the body-mind). The mind has become quiet means that it has surrendered to the experience of Self, the truth. When the mind (ego) realizes that it only needs to bow down, then it will surrender due to love and devotion. It is then that Self becomes aware of Self. Bliss alone manifests.

There is a difference between the mind chattering and the mind singing devotional hymns. When the mind sings devotional hymns in praise for Self, the feeling of surrender will intensify. The chattering of the mind indicates that there is lack of understanding, or there is some confusion. The chattering of the mind itself is the cause of all trouble. Due to this chattering, the mind becomes restless and keeps running either in the past or the future. However, when the mind sings hymns, then it indicates that something has happened with it, it is beginning to understand some things. Bright love towards Self is awakening within. If this is happening, rest assured that a lot is happening. If you are in this state even for a short while, understand that this is the right state. Now your feet are free from bondage, your ears have opened, and your eyes are opening. This is the state of stillness. It is this supreme silence from where thoughts arise and into which thoughts dissolve. There is no such thing as bringing in a thoughtless state. You will understand through practice that the state of thoughtlessness is already there. It has always been there, right from the beginning. It is in this state that things (imaginations) rise and fall. Hence, do not be under the belief that thoughts should not occur. Thoughts will occur at any time. They will come in order to carry out some action through your body. But you are only witnessing these thoughts. You will remain an onlooker or witness to your thoughts. You must have the conviction that you are already in a thoughtless state, a state of silence, whether you are still or moving around.

Q. 7: Why has God created mind in humans? If He has made the mind, how can it be eliminated?

A: A demon once ardently worshipped the Lord in order to please Him. Pleased with his worship, the Lord granted a boon to the demon. The boon was as per what he wished for - whatever he places his hand on will be destroyed.

On receiving the boon, the demon thought, "To test this power that I have received, why don't I try it first on the Lord Himself!" The thought was trying to know the Source from which it emerged. It wanted to see its own creator. It is just like a wave that wishes to know the sea, thinking itself as a separate entity. Similarly, the demon told the Lord, "If I keep my hand on your head, it will prove whether the blessing you have given me is effective or not." Now, the Lord vanished. This means that when the mind tries to know the experience of Self, the experience vanishes.

The demon chased the Lord and the Lord kept eluding him. The Lord then disguised Himself as a beautiful dancer. When the demon looked at her, he was charmed by her beauty. He mimicked the gestures and expressions performed by the dancer. While dancing, the dancer placed her hand on her head. The demon, who was imitating her gestures, also kept his hand on his head and was immediately burnt to ashes.

Through this story, understand: How and when the demon turns into ashes and dies? When is this state achieved and why does the Lord keep eluding him? What is the reason behind all this? In the story, the Lord symbolizes Self (the experience of beingness) and the demon symbolizes the mind. The mind wants to see the Lord (Self). It never wants to remain still and silent. The demon could have lived happily with the blessing, but he turned his blessing into a curse. He misused it. The Lord made the mind (demon) place its hands on itself, i.e. when the mind enquires about itself, it drops.

The mind always goes astray in false happiness. It never wants to die. The mind repeatedly tries to see the experience of Self. The more the mind runs after it, the more the experience of beingness eludes it. When the mind and thoughts are absent, the experience of beingness alone is there. As soon as thoughts appear, the experience of beingness disappears. Just as, after you wake up in the morning, many thoughts arise in the mind due to which the experience of beingness that was present throughout the night vanishes. Actually, it does not vanish; it is always present. But, it is obscured by the mind.

God did not create the human mind thinking of it as a bad thing. Mind was not a bad thing for God, but the characteristic trait of this mind is that it always divides everything into two. To understand the mind, the mind itself has to be used. The Lord did not grant the boon to the demon thinking of it as a bad thing. But eventually it (the mind) became an obstacle. When the demon placed his hand on himself, he was destroyed. That means, when the mind doubts the credibility of itself, it shifts its focus from others onto itself. It is due to this self-examination that the mind becomes ready to die.

'Good' or 'bad' is the language of the mind. When God created the mind, he did not intend anything good or bad. The mind was created only for Self to experience Self. Understand this with another example.

A man was playing chess with himself from both sides of the chess board. You told him, "Don't kill any of the pieces." He replied, "Then what is the fun of playing this game? A mistake will be made from one side and from the other side a chess-piece will be slain. Only then will the game continue, and there can be some enjoyment." This implies that from all sides, Self alone is experiencing Self. But the mind considers itself as a separate entity, a doer. This belief of the mind to be a separate entity is the cause of all troubles. When the understanding will dawn that the one making you complain is also the same Self, the ego of the mind will then shatter. As the ego dissolves, it becomes crystal clear that the division of everything into 'good' or 'bad' was part of the mind's game only.

Q. 8: What understanding must the mind receive to attain the experience of Self?

A: A chief executive officer (CEO) of a company was sitting in his cabin. Some people came to meet him and asked the secretary if they could go in. The secretary went in to check if he was available.

The secretary had worn a very strong perfume which made the CEO faint in his chair as soon as she entered the cabin. Thinking that he was tired and taking some rest, she came out of the cabin and told the visitors that the CEO was resting for a while. She asked them to wait. The moment she came out of the cabin, the effect of the perfume wore off, and the CEO woke up and continued with his work.

After a little while, when she entered his cabin again to check, again he fainted. When she came out of the cabin, he woke up. This continued several times over. After waiting for a very long time, the visitors insisted her to check one more time. Baffled by what was happening the secretary ultimately came to understand that it was because of her that the CEO was falling unconscious. Once she understood this, she asked the visitors to go in directly. She realized that there was no need for her to check.

When the secretary finally understood that her presence was making her boss unconscious, she stopped going in front of the boss. Similarly, the mind must also understand that when it goes and checks for the experience of Self, the attention is in the head. Just as the checking of the secretary was the cause of the CEO's unconsciousness, likewise the constant checking of the mind hides the experience of truth.

The mind always wants to check the experience of beingness. That is why the experience of beingness disappears. The mind and the experience of beingness can never co-exist together. Either the checker can remain or the experience of beingness. The crux of the matter is that either the mind will remain, or the experience of beingness! Both cannot come face-to-face. The mind feels, "Just as I have been seeing everything else, I must also see the experience of beingness." But it must understand as soon as possible that only in its absence can Self experience Self. Then it will get ready to surrender and drop.

❖ ❖ ❖

You can send your opinion or feedback on this book to:

Tej Gyan Foundation, P.O. Box 25, Pimpri Colony,
Pimpri, Pune – 411017, Maharashtra, INDIA
Email: englishbooks@tejgyan.org

Write for Us
We welcome writers, translators and editors to join our team. If you would like to volunteer, please email us at: englishbooks@tejgyan.org or call: +91 90110 10963

APPENDICES

About Sirshree

Sirshree's spiritual quest, which began during his childhood, led him on a journey through various schools of thought and prevalent meditation practices. His overpowering desire to attain the Truth made him relinquish his teaching profession. After a long period of contemplation on the truth of life, his spiritual quest culminated in the attainment of the ultimate truth. Since then, over the last two decades, he has dedicated his life toward elevating mass consciousness and making spiritual pursuit simple and accessible to all.

Sirshree espouses, "**All paths that lead to the truth begin differently, but culminate at the same point – understanding. Understanding is complete in itself. Listening to this understanding is enough to attain the truth.**"

Sirshree has delivered more than 3000 discourses that throw light on this understanding, simplify various aspects of life and unravel missing links in spirituality. He delivers the understanding in casual contemporary language by weaving profound aspects into analogies, parables and humor that provoke one to contemplate.

To make it possible for people from all walks of life to directly experience this understanding, Sirshree has designed the *Maha Aasmani Param Gyan Shivir* – a retreat designed as a comprehensive system for imparting wisdom. This system for wisdom, which has been accredited with ISO 9001:2015 certification, has inspired thousands of seekers from all walks of life to progress on their journey of the Truth. This system makes the wisdom accessible to every human being, regardless of religion, caste, social strata, country or belief system.

Sirshree is the founder of Tej Gyan Foundation, a no-profit organization committed to raising mass consciousness with branches in India, the United States, Europe and Asia-Pacific. Sirshree's retreats have transformed the lives of thousands and his teachings have inspired various social initiatives for raising global consciousness.

His published work includes more than 100 books, some of which have been translated in more than 10 languages and published by leading publishers. Sirshree's books provide profound and practical reading on existential subjects like emotional maturity, harmony in relationships, developing self-belief, overcoming stress and anxiety, and dealing with the question of life-beyond-death, to name a few. His literature on core spirituality expounds the deeper meaning of self-realization and self-stabilization, unravelling missing links in the understanding of karma, wisdom, devotion, meditation and consciousness.

Various luminaries and celebrities like His Holiness the Dalai Lama, publishers Mr. Reid Tracy, Ms. Tami Simon and Yoga Master Dr. B. K. S. Iyengar have released Sirshree's books and lauded his work. "The Source" book series, authored by Sirshree, has sold over 10 million copies in 5 years. His book, "The Warrior's Mirror", published by Penguin, was featured in the Limca Book of Records for being released on the same day in 11 languages.

Tejgyan... The Road Ahead
What is Tejgyan?

Tejgyan is the wisdom of the existential truth, which is beyond duality. "Gyan" is a term commonly used for "knowledge". Tejgyan is the wisdom beyond knowledge and ignorance. It is understanding that arises from direct experience of the final truth. It is what sets us free from the limitations of the mind and opens us to our highest potential.

In today's world, there are people who feel disharmony and are desperately trying to achieve balance in an unpredictable life. Tejgyan helps them in harmonizing with their true nature, the Self, thereby restoring balance in all aspects of their lives.

And then, there are those who are successful, but feel a sense of emptiness within. Tejgyan provides them fulfilment and helps them to embark on a journey towards self-realization. There are others who feel lost and are seeking the meaning of life. Tejgyan helps them to realize the true purpose of human life.

All this is possible with Tejgyan due to a very simple reason. The experience of the ultimate truth (God or Pure consciousness) is always available. The direct experience of this truth is possible provided the right method is known. Tejgyan is that method, that understanding.

The understanding of Tejgyan makes it possible to lead a life of freedom from fear, worry, anger and stress. It helps in attaining physical vitality, emotional strength and stability, harmony in relationships, financial freedom and spiritual progress.

At Tej Gyan Foundation, Sirshree imparts this understanding through a System for Wisdom – a series of retreats that guides participants step by step towards realizing the true Self, being established in the experience of self-realization, and expressing its qualities. This system for wisdom has been accredited with the ISO 9001:2015 certification.

Maha Aasmani Param Gyan Shivir

"**Maha Aasmani Param Gyan Shivir**" is the flagship Self-realization retreat offered by Tej Gyan Foundation. The retreat is conducted in Hindi. The teachings of the retreat are non-denominational (secular).

This residential retreat is held for 3 to 5 days at the foundation's MaNaN

Ashram amidst the glory of the mountains and the pristine beauty of nature. The Ashram is located at the outskirts of the city of Pune in India, and is well connected by air, road and rail. The retreat is also held at other centres of Tej Gyan Foundation across the world.

You can participate in this retreat to attain ageless wisdom through a unique System for Wisdom so that you can:

- Discover "Who am I" through direct experience.
- Learn to abide in pure consciousness while functioning in the world, allowing the qualities of consciousness like peace, love, joy, compassion, abundance and creativity to manifest.
- Acquire simple tools to use in everyday life, which help quiet the chattering mind.
- Get practical techniques to be in the present and connect to the source of all answers within (the inner guru).
- Discover missing links in the practices of Meditation (*Dhyana*), Action (*Karma*), Wisdom (*Gyana*) and Devotion (*Bhakti*).
- Understand the nature of your body-mind mechanism to attain freedom form its tendencies.
- Learn practical methods to shift from mind-centered living to consciousness-centered living.

A Mini-retreat is also conducted, especially for teenagers (14 to 16 years of age) during summer and winter vacations.

To register for retreats, visit www.tejgyan.org,
contact (+91) 9921008060, or email mail@tejgyan.com

MaNaN Ashram

Survey No. 43, Sanas Nagar, Nandoshi gaon, Kirkatwadi Phata, Sinhagad Road, Dist. Pune 411024, Maharashtra, India.

Now you can register online for
the following retreats

Maha Aasmani Param Gyan Shivir
(5 Days Residential Retreat in Hindi)

Mini Maha Aasmani Shivir
3 Days (Residential) Retreat for Teens

🔍 www.tejgyan.org

Books can be delivered at your doorstep by registered post or courier. You can request the same through postal money order or pay by VPP. Please send the money order to either of the following two addresses:

WOW Publishings Pvt. Ltd.

1. Registered Office: E-4, Vaibhav Nagar, Near Tapovan Mandir, Pimpri, Pune - 411017.

2. Post Box No. 36, Pimpri Colony Post Office, Pimpri, Pune - 411017

Phone No: (+91) 9011013210 / 9623457873

You can also order your copy at the online store:

www.gethappythoughts.org

*Free Shipping plus 10% Discount on purchases above Rs. 500/-

About Tej Gyan Foundation

Tej Gyan Foundation (TGF) was established with the mission of creating a highly evolved society through all-round development of every individual that transforms all the facets of their lives. It is a non-profit organization, founded on the teachings of Sirshree.

The Foundation has received the ISO certification (ISO 9001:2015) for its system of imparting wisdom. It has centres all across India as well as in other countries. The motto of Tej Gyan Foundation is 'Happy Thoughts'.

At the core of the philosophy of Tejgyan is the Power of Acceptance. Acceptance has profound meaning and is at the core of our Being. It is Acceptance that brings forth true love, joy and peace.

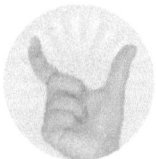

Symbol of Acceptance

The Symbol of Acceptance – shown above – is a representation of this truth. The symbol represents brackets. Whatever occurs in life falls within these brackets that signify acceptance of whatever *is*. Hence, this symbol forms the centerpiece of the Foundation's MaNaN Ashram.

The Foundation is creating a highly evolved society through:

- Tejgyan Programs (Retreats, YouTube Webcasts)
- Tejgyan Books and Apps
- Tejgyan Projects (Value education, Women empowerment, Peace initiatives)

The Foundation undertakes projects to elevate the level of consciousness among students, youth, women, senior citizens, teachers, doctors, leaders, professionals, corporate and Government organizations, police force, prisoners etc.

For further details contact:
Tejgyan Global Foundation
Registered Office:
Happy Thoughts Building, Vikrant Complex, Near Tapovan Mandir, Pimpri, Pune 411017, Maharashtra, India.
Contact No: 020-27411240, 27412576
Email: mail@tejgyan.com

MaNaN Ashram:
Survey No. 43, Sanas Nagar, Nandoshi gaon, Kirkatwadi Phata, Sinhagad Road, Tal. Haveli, Dist. Pune 411024, Maharashtra, India.
Contact No: 992100 8060.

Hyderabad: 9885558100, **Bangalore:** 9880412588, **Delhi :** 9891059875, **Nashik:** 9326967980, **Mumbai:** 9373440985

For accessing our unique 'System for Wisdom' from self-help to self-realization, please follow us on:

	Website Online Shopping/ Blog	www.tejgyan.org www.gethappythoughts.org
	Video Channel	www.youtube.com/tejgyan For Q&A videos: http://goo.gl/YA81DQ
	Social networking	www.facebook.com/tejgyan
	Social networking	www.twitter.com/sirshree
	Internet Radio	http://www.tejgyan.org/internetradio.aspx

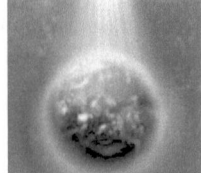

Pray for World Peace along with thousands of others every day at 09:09am and 09:09pm

Divine Light of Love, Bliss and Peace is Showering;
The Golden Light of Higher Consciousness is Rising;
All negativity on Earth is Dissolving;
Everyone is in Peace and Blissfully Shining;
O God, Gratitude for Everything!

www.ingramcontent.com/pod-product-compliance
Lightning Source LLC
LaVergne TN
LVHW040146080526
838202LV00042B/3038